SWEETHEART
CHRISTMAS

MINDY HARDWICK

EAGLE BAY PRESS

Story Blurb

I vy dreads the holiday season. But this year promises to be even worse as her brother, and only family, will not be returning home for the holidays. Ivy is doing her best to avoid all festivities. But with the tree lighting, a holiday homes tour, and the downtown door decorating contest, it's hard to skip the holidays in Cranberry Bay. Meanwhile after his grandfather dies, Josh must step into Cranberry Bay's beloved holiday tradition to drive the Holiday Express Christmas Eve train. When he asks Ivy to play the role of Mrs. Claus neither expects their long-time friendship to turn into love.

Contents

PRINT ISBN: 979-8-218-23169-9
October 2023

Developmental Editor: Bev Katz Rosenbaum
Copy Editor: Heart Full of Ink, Casey Harris-Parks
Cover Artist: Su Kopil, Earthly Charms
Book Format and Layout: Eagle Bay Press

Eagle Bay Press
P.O. Box 1391
Cannon Beach, Oregon. 97110

For the Rose City RWA Monday Night Sprint Group whose weekly support kept me writing during the pandemic.

Cast of Characters

Shuster Family

Rebecca: Mother of the Shuster Family. Widowed. Retired librarian.

Sawyer: Oldest brother. Land Developer. Married to Katie

Lauren: Sawyer's daughter. Ten-years-old. Mother died of cancer.

Bryan Shuster. Middle Brother. Real Estate agent. Married to Rylee.

Adam Shuster: Youngest Brother. Park Ranger. Friends with Josh Morton.

Lisa Shuster: Single mother to daughter Maddie. Lives in carriage house on Sawyer's property.

Maddie: Sixteen-year-old daughter of Lisa.

<u>Sewing Circle</u>

Katie Coos: Owns the Fabric and Sewing Barn. Married to Sawyer

Rylee Harper: Owns the River Cottages. Married to Bryan, her childhood sweetheart. Owns Raisin. a mixed brown and white mutt.

Ivy Moore: Owns the Red Door Antique Shop.

Gracie Catskill: Owns the River Rock Inn.

Sasha Frazier: Owns the Lazy Dayz Bakery. Mother of Tyler

Tyler: Ten-year old son of Sasha.

Chapter 1

Ivy screwed a lightbulb inside the body of the vintage, plastic, three-foot Santa. She placed it on the counter and plugged the cord into an outlet. The glowing Santa lit the festive holiday pins inside the glass case. The green, red, silver, and gold pins sparkled. Ivy grabbed a key from a hook alongside the outlet and slipped it into the lock. She turned the key and twisted the round knob to the left. The wood door slid open, and she adjusted the white cloth around the pins.

"Beautiful." A woman with jet black hair peered into the counter. "My Grandmother always wore a red and green tree pin every Christmas day."

Ivy swallowed. Her mom always wore a pin, too. When she died, Ivy made sure to take the wreath pin from her mom's jewelry box before she and her brother were taken away. She kept that pin tucked in a sock as she and her brother were shuffled from foster home to foster home. Until one day, she arrived home from school to find it had been stolen, sold by one of the other foster kids who needed it for drug money. She'd spent hours scouring eBay but it never turned up. The magic of Christmas dissolved without her mom, and the holiday became a day to endure, not enjoy.

Once she was sure the lighted Santa's bulb worked, Ivy unplugged the Santa. She placed it in a large cardboard box beside the counter. Lifting the pen from a Mason jar of pens, she checked the box on a printed checklist. Three sheets of to-do lists were stacked on the clipboard. Each item described in detail what was needed to pull off a successful holiday season at her Red Door Antique store. She saw no reason in getting sentimental over the Christmas holidays. It was just another event, no different than the summer celebrations or the fall harvest festival the town put on every year.

"Can I show you one of the pins?" Ivy asked, making sure her voice gave away no hint of emotion.

"The pins are beautiful, and I wish I was buying one." The woman shook her head. "But I came to buy tickets to the Holiday Homes Tour. I'd like four."

Ivy closed the door to the pin counter and grabbed a thick manila envelope sitting on the counter behind her. She flipped open the folder and pulled out four Holiday Homes Tour tickets.

"The tickets are wonderful." The woman turned one of the gold tickets over in her hand. "They are so beautifully designed."

"Thank you." Ivy tucked the folder away. The Holiday Homes Tour was one of the signature events in

Cranberry Bay's Hometown Holidays extravaganza. The Cranberry Bay Business Association prided itself on the historic homes tour. Rooms in the town's bed and breakfast, boutique inn, and riverside cottages were booked out for months. And those who couldn't get rooms in Cranberry Bay enjoyed nearby seaside town hotels with warm gas fireplaces and views overlooking a stormy Pacific Ocean.

The Red Door Antique Shop was a proud sponsor of the Holiday Homes Tour and Ivy worked hard each year to make sure it was a success. The same ten homes were always invited to participate, and it went off without a hitch—with the exception of the year when three of the homes declined invitations due to a pending home sale, the death of a homeowner, and a remodel. Ivy rubbed her temples. That holiday season still gave her a headache.

Ivy noted the six boxes lined up alongside the counter. She consulted her checklist. Every year, she prepared the same boxes for the home decorations, from pink and red vintage glass ornaments to old-fashioned three-foot plastic Santas. Of course, people muttered about how the homes looked the same year after year, and the tour had grown a little stale in the last two years, but she ignored the complaints. Holidays were supposed to be filled with tradition. Traditions stayed the same, that's what made them tradition. And the important thing was each year, she was given a certificate at the Business Association's Annual Year-End Awards Ceremony for her work on the tour. She hung the certificates in a row alongside her first-place award for the business's downtown decorating contest. Ten of the framed certificates hung down the hallway leading to her small office. Each one of the awards and certificates reminding her that she did belong to the small community of Cranberry Bay, despite arriving as a child in foster care.

Ivy wrapped a cord around a small tabletop lighted Santa and chuckled at the small bite on Santa's beard. Her year-old spaniel mix, Max, sprawled across his bed under a rolltop desk. He was both a blessing and terror, trying her patience with his constant chewing and bringing her laughter and joy with his puppy charm. She never dreamed of owning a pet, but Max arrived as a small puppy, wrapped in a blanket and placed near the shop's dumpster. She brought him inside, gave him a warm spot in her bed that night, and intended to take him to the animal shelter the next day. But he'd won her over, curled up beside her, and she didn't have the heart to let him go. Unfortunately, he also needed some training.

The door to the antique shop opened and a gust of wind caught it as ten-year-old Tyler and his Mom, Sasha, walked into the store, each carrying a large tray with an assortment of holiday cookies. The woman with the Holiday Homes ticket ducked out of the shop and into the gusty day.

"Try one, Ivy." Tyler set a plate of cookies on the counter. He wore a knit stocking cap, a down jacket, and jeans. He dipped his finger into a glob of icing on the plate and licked it off. "This is the best icing!"

Sasha set the plate of frosted Santas beside the tree cookies. Her red jacket hung open and revealed a holiday sweater with a festive, decorated Christmas tree that dropped to black leggings, and a pair of knee-high boots completed the outfit. A set of sparkling Christmas trees hung from her ears.

"We've been having a debate," Sasha said. "We each tried a little different dough mix. Now we need to know which one is the best."

"Mine, of course." Tyler dropped to the floor beside Max and rubbed him behind his long ears. "I'm working on a special holiday treat for Max."

Sasha tossed back her head and laughed. She ruffled Tyler's hair. "He's going to take over the bakery for me one day and I'll retire."

Ivy winked at her friend. "I don't see retirement in your future for a long time." At thirty, Sasha was filled with life and spunk, churning out breads, pastries, cookies, and her specialty sandwiches for the town.

"Speaking of retirement…" Sasha leaned across the counter and picked up one of the shiny pink glass vintage ornaments. She placed it in a small box alongside two other vintage ornaments. "How are Rick and Laura?"

"Enjoying Santa Fe," Ivy said. "Laura sent me pictures of the luminaires. It's been their dream to spend the Christmas season in Santa Fe. I'm glad it's finally happening."

Ivy clicked the last text she'd gotten from Laura and pushed her phone toward Sasha. Ivy missed her foster parents, but she knew that traveling in their RV was exactly what the two planned to do with their retirement. Both worked hard, Rick as the town's long-time postmaster and Laura in what used to be the antique shop, a store of cluttered items no one could find any use for anymore. When Rick retired, Laura wanted to sell the shop, but Ivy offered to run it. She'd been helping in the shop since she came to live with Rick and Laura as a thirteen-year-old. As Laura aged, she wanted fewer hours at the Antique Shop. Ivy easily took over the hours and found she enjoyed taking in items no one wanted and figuring out a way to repurpose them. The reuse movement was gathering steam, and with her keen design eye, she'd created small rooms using petition boards where independent vendors could sell their antique items. She also opened a storefront online and found that what other people thought of as junk and collections they couldn't use anymore fetched a good sum of money. Her love of visual design paid off in both her shop and the marketing designs she created and soon business was brisk.

"Is Keith coming home for Christmas?" Sasha nudged the phone back to Ivy.

"He took the Christmas shift," Ivy said, trying hard not to let the sadness fill her chest. She always spent Christmas with her twin brother, through all the foster homes and their childhood, they always made a pledge to spend Christmas together. But his police job in a small town north of Seattle needed him. "He took the shift so his partner could be home with his family on Christmas. They have two small children who are very excited about Christmas."

"You can't be alone for Christmas," Sasha placed her hands on her hips. "Tyler and I would love to have you join—"

Bells jingled as the door to the Red Door Antiques opened. "I've got room in the truck for one more box." Josh's blue eyes sparkled, and his Santa hat tilted at an angle. Curly dark hair framed his face. He wore a red holiday sweater with twinkle lights, dark blue jeans, and work boots.

"This one goes to Mrs. Perkins on Hemlock Street." Ivy toed the box by her foot. She checked a box on her clipboard beside Jan Perkin's name. "I think she must have a hundred Santas. Every year, she requests another box." She smiled at her long-time friend, Josh Morton. Josh and her brother Keith were her constant companions in high school. During her senior year, she'd been paired with him for the school's holiday food drive. During the food drive, he encouraged her to sign up to be one of the elves for the town's annual Holiday Express Christmas Eve train—a small train his grandfather owned and drove. Eager to spend more time close to Josh and her bubbling feelings for him, she'd signed up. As the train chugged toward the pretend North Pole, they worked together, serving hot cocoa and making sure the children were settled in their seats.

As the children disembarked the train, Josh pulled her under a small twig of mistletoe he held above her head and kissed her briefly on the lips. She spent the entire Christmas vacation dreaming of Josh and how they would marry, have children, and stay in Cranberry Bay forever. But, when she'd returned to school in January, she found his sister's best friend, Kami, staked claims on him at a New Year's Eve party, and the two quickly formed what everyone called the perfect match. A match which lasted through their senior year, college, and into adulthood. This fall, Kami took a job in Seattle, but everyone still expected Josh to propose to his long-time high school sweetheart this holiday season.

Although Ivy pulled away from Josh as much as possible, not wanting to allow her feelings toward him to ruin a long-time friendship, Josh and Keith's friendship remained strong after high school. The two often included her on hikes, day trips to Portland, and even a couple kayak lessons. She always made sure to remind herself to keep her feelings tucked deep inside. She never wanted to ruin the friendship between the three of them. When Keith announced he wasn't coming home this Christmas, Josh stepped forward and offered to watch out for Ivy during the holidays. He'd be her big brother while her big brother was absent this season. Josh wouldn't take the place of Keith, but it was nice to have his help, especially with the Holiday Homes Tour. Her friendship with Josh was much more important than mooning over a high school crush fantasy because of a one-time kiss. A kiss he'd most likely long forgotten.

Josh opened a small bag and held out dog reindeer antlers. "I brought something for Max."

He strode around the counter and leaned down to the dog who stood, shook himself off, and wagged his back end at Josh. Josh placed the reindeer antlers on Max's head.

He straightened and eyed Ivy. "Where's your festive spirit?"

Ivy flushed. She wore the same thing every weekend. A pair of black slacks, a black turtleneck sweater, and a simple paisley scarf draped around her neck. There wasn't a hint of red and green on her.

"Ivy!" Rylee burst into the shop. Her dog, Raisin, bounded in after her, soaking wet. He shook and water sprayed across the room and dampened a set of vintage holiday cards displayed on a small metal rack. Rylee wore a dark raincoat over jeans and red boots. She'd returned to Cranberry Bay a couple years ago and married her high school sweetheart, Bryan. The two ran the River Rock Cottages, and Bryan worked as the town real estate agent.

Max dashed from behind the counter and barked at Raisin before racing after him, down the small aisle of the shop. Items crashed to the floor in their wake with thuds and a glass dish shattered. Tyler leaped to his feet and followed Max and Raisin, shouting at the top of his lungs for both the dogs.

Josh knocked against the box of Santas and three rolled out as he raced after the two dogs. "Max! Raisin!"

"He's not on a leash!" Ivy turned to Rylee.

"I'm so sorry!" Rylee held up a long leather leash. "We were just in the pet store next door and Paige allows all dogs to be off leash. The door opened and he ran out. We were lucky he ran into your store!" Rylee shuddered.

"I would hate to see him run toward the river and across the road!" She pointed outside as a large truck lumbered past the shop.

A loud crash came from the back of the store. Josh hollered, "I got them!"

Ivy gritted her teeth. Ever since Paige moved her dog shop next door and took the place of Ivy's long-time friend, Katie's fabric shop, Paige wanted to take over the Cranberry Bay Business Association with all her new ideas. Ideas that pushed Ivy to the side of the Business Association where she'd made her name in the town.

Ivy pointed to the large sign she hung on her front window. "All dogs must be leashed."

But no one noticed as Rylee and Sasha raced down the aisle after Raisin. Ivy followed behind, picking up one item after another which were knocked out of the vendor's spaces in Raisin's run.

"You got him!" Ivy said to Josh, who lay across a table, holding onto each dog's collar with both hands. The white lace tablecloth sprawled on the ground, dirty with paw prints, and a stack of old-fashioned cookie tins lay on the floor, but the rest of station #657 looked to be intact. Ivy exhaled. Perfectly groomed, Amy Beth Miller, station #657, inspected her area every Saturday. She never lowered prices. She usually raised them and then announced a sale with a small pink sign. Ivy glanced at the pink antique tabletop clock. Amy Beth Miller was due to arrive at any minute.

And then as if on cue, Amy Beth's light voice carried

down the store as her boot heels clicked on the floors. "Do I smell wet dog?"

She took two more steps and turned the corner. Her loud gasp filled the area. "What is going on?" Amy Beth raised her eyebrows, and she shook her head. Her bobbed, frosted hair bounced on her shoulders.

Ivy grabbed hold of Max's collar. "We were just trying to round up the dogs."

"Why are there dogs in my area?" She placed her hands on her hips and tapped her high heeled black boot against the hardwood floor.

"They're getting Santa pictures," Rylee said brightly. "It's Paws for a Cause."

"Here?" Amy Beth turned around in a slow circle.

"Yes!" Josh sat up on the table and straightened his Santa hat.

Mary Beth eyed Josh. "You are not dressed like Santa. You don't have a beard, the suit, or the stomach."

"He's one of Santa's helpers," Rylee took Raisin's collar and, with her knee, maneuvered him so he stood on her left side.

Josh hopped off the table and straightened his shirt. He grabbed onto the collar of Max. "I'll escort him back to his spot at the front. Tyler, can you help me out? Maybe coax him with a bit of your fabulous cookies."

Tyler pulled out a bit of cookie crumb from his pocket and held it out to Max who followed behind, trailing after the cookie crumbs.

"He's a regular pied piper," Sasha followed after

Tyler. "Just as long as he doesn't mention the word dog to me for Christmas again."

"I heard you," Tyler said, his voice loud.

Sasha shook her head and a smile lit her face.

Ivy followed Josh, Sasha, Tyler, Max, Rylee, and Raisin down the aisle with Mary Beth hollering after them, "I'll expect all this to be taken off the bill for renting my space, Ivy."

Ivy grimaced. Mary Beth never wanted to pay the full monthly price for her space. She found every reason she could to get a discount, even though she was the best-selling vendor.

Ivy grabbed her holiday homes clipboard. The small squares and ordered list calmed her stomach. "We should be able to wrap this up in another hour. There are two more boxes of Santas and one box of vintage ornaments to deliver. I can get the rest in my car."

"I'll help you," Josh said. "My truck can fit everything in one trip." He leaned against the counter and grabbed one of the holiday Santa cookies.

"Try mine!" Tyler pushed the tray of tree cookies to him.

"I'll take one of each." Josh winked at Tyler.

"I've got a basket of gifts for the holiday train," Rylee said. On Christmas Eve, the Holiday Express would glide up to the Cranberry Bay station and blow the steam whistle, calling all the children aboard for hot cocoa and a magic ride to see Santa, who waited at the end of the line with a small gift for each child. Gifts which were donated by the local townspeople and wrapped in colorful wrapping. Books, coloring books, crayons, small dolls, and toys. The tradition was fifty years old and grown adults still held onto their prized toys or books from the Holiday Express. Ivy kept a small toy chest of gifts from the Holiday Express at the front of the store. But most of the time it was empty. Families just didn't give away their childhood gifts from the Holiday Express.

"I'll stop by later today," Josh said, his voice deepened.

Without thinking, Ivy reached out and touched his arm. "I can help you." She knew that losing his grandfather last summer hadn't been easy and this would be the first season the Holiday Express would run without its long-time owner. The weight of carrying on the beloved tradition was now on Josh's shoulders.

She wasn't the only one missing a beloved family member at the holidays. Josh needed someone to be there for him, too, as a friend. Josh's eyes met hers and a small tremor of warmth filled her. She quickly brushed it away as nothing more than a look good friends exchange.

Chapter 2

Josh opened the refrigerator and placed his Tupperware container inside. He made sure to leave enough space for the other Fir Pine Elementary School teachers who also used the staff refrigerator. As an early riser, Josh arrived at school before anyone else. He enjoyed the quirkiness of the early, historic nineteen-hundreds, three story elementary school building. The wood floors creaked and groaned. The heater clunked and sounded like it might grumble to a complete stop. The winter rain pounded on the large windows in each room.

A red and green December staff duty calendar hung on the bulletin board underneath a cherry letter banner. Last month, he'd been in charge of morning bus drop-off, herding the elementary students from their buses into the cafeteria for steaming bowls of oatmeal, cinnamon rolls, and pancakes. Fir Pine Elementary was lucky to have Steve and Jeremiah working in the cafeteria, best friends since their own days at Fir Pine Elementary. Both were determined to give the students a warm start to their school day, knowing so many of the children who attended Fir Pine didn't have three hot meals a day. Josh located his name on the duty calendar listed under the after-school parent pick-up duty. The after-school parent pick-up could be a bit chaotic. Everyone gathered in the library, and he often used the time to browse for new books to read to his second-grade class.

"Good morning." Caitlin Gobskin pushed open the faculty room door. The petite fifth grade teacher sashed by Josh. She carried a large box with the Lazy Dayz bakery emblem on the side. "The furnace sounds like it's not going to make it to lunch. Do you remember the year when the furnace broke and no one could fix it for what seemed like weeks?"

"Fifth grade!" Josh said. "I think I lived in my puffy green coat that year."

"Kami and I kept a warmer in our desk and passed it back and forth. It worked fine until the battery died when we left it on overnight."

"You were lucky nothing caught fire," Josh said.

"Mr. Johnson found it when he was cleaning the class-room." Caitlin shook her head. "We were lucky."

Kami and Caitlin had been best friends since elemen-tary school. In middle school, the two joined the commu-nity swim team and met his sister, Suzanne, who was a year ahead of them. The three became fast friends, and Kami and Caitlin would often be found hanging out in his sister's room, listening to music and pouring over teen fashion videos. When Kami invited him to the New Year's Eve party his senior year of high school, it seemed like the entire party waited for them to kiss. He never told anyone that the kiss didn't feel the same as the one he gave to Ivy under the mistletoe on the Holiday Express a few weeks earlier. The kiss he and Ivy never talked about again. And then he and Kami were just a couple, a comfortable couple who'd known each other since elementary school and who everyone expected would be married and settle in Cranberry Bay to raise their family in one of the Craftsman homes lining the bluff over-looking the river. An expectation that cracked when Kami took the job in Seattle this past August.

"Have you heard from Kami lately?" Caitlin asked as if she read his mind.

Josh shook his head. "Not since Halloween." He didn't tell Caitlin that he called Kami on Halloween, expecting her to be at home answering the door to trick-or-treaters like she always enjoyed at her childhood home in Cranberry Bay. Instead, she answered in the middle of a party.

"My boss treated us to a spooky corn field," she said as a male voice in what sounded like he was so close he was pressed against her said, "Is that a ghost?"

"I gotta go. I'll call you later." Kami had quickly clicked off the phone.

But later didn't happen. Josh didn't expect it to. They'd been on rocky grounds all summer, and when she left for her new job in Seattle, both decided that it would be best to take a break. At first, both of them tried to keep in contact, quick texts with a funny meme or emoji. Then the texts trickled off to nothing. He thought he would feel sad, but instead he felt relief. Relief he didn't have to keep pretending to be in love with someone who he wasn't in love with.

Now, it was just a matter of waiting to see who would publicly announce the break-up, neither wanting to field the questions and concerns and kindhearted well-meaning remarks that were sure to come at them from every corner of Cranberry Bay. Josh knew he would take the brunt of their break-up, still living in Cranberry Bay. He'd seen what happened to his friend, Adam Shuster, when he broke it off with his long-time high school girl-friend, who decided to travel and just never returned to Cranberry Bay. Adam hadn't been involved with anyone since, not wanting to risk the endless casseroles that showed up at his cabin at the entrance to the state park or the women's hiking groups who invited him along, just for companionship, all of them vying for his attention and heart. Cranberry Bay loved their high school sweethearts turned husband and wife couples and struggled to let go when those couples didn't work out.

Josh followed Caitlin to the table in the center of the room.

She placed the box on the table and threw back the lid. "Early bird gets the best croissant!"

Josh licked his lips and pulled out a chocolate crois-sant coated with powdered sugar.

"I know," Caitlin shrugged. "Not the healthiest way to start the morning, but it's December. We'll all be eating unhealthily all month. Next month we can bring back the morning fruit and granola."

At 5'5 and an avid biker, Caitlin worked off calories as fast as Josh. They often biked together along the winding streets of Cranberry Bay in the early morning hours when the sun was just peaking up over the coast mountain range. Sometimes, Jill, the school nurse, and Mike, one of the fourth-grade teachers, joined them. Josh enjoyed a beer after work with Mike sometimes and knew he was trying to get to know Jill better. But so far, Jill hadn't taken any of Mike's hints.

Josh slipped a colorful flyer from the back of his clipboard and tacked it carefully to the staff announcements.

"The Holiday Express!" Caitlin said, her voice rising six octaves. "My daughter can't wait to go. This is her first year riding the train."

Josh smiled at Caitlin and her excitement. He pushed down the wave of sorrow that rose inside his stomach. Every year since he'd been a child, his grandfather drove the Holiday Express. The old steam engine was his grandfather's passion. After Josh became too old to believe in Santa, he helped wrap and load the toys into the thick bags. As the train chugged toward the imaginary North Pole, Josh moved between the train cars, making the children laugh with his elf costume, and then on the way home, checking on each child to see that the toy they received was the perfect one for them. This year the role of conductor would fall to him. His grandfather trained him to drive the steam engine for the last year. He knew he could drive the train, but he wasn't sure he was ready to step into the role his grandfather played for the town for over fifty years.

"Here's the toy drive announcement." Tricia, the school office manager, breezed into the faculty room and attached a second flyer beside Josh's. Tricia served on the train's non-profit board and worked with the volunteer firefighters of Cranberry Bay to help coordinate all the donations. She'd been married to the Fire Chief for fifteen years and enjoyed helping distribute the gifts by volunteering as one of the train's elves on Christmas Eve.

"What's that delicious smell?" Anne Marks strode through the door, her walkie-talkie crackling at her side as the school buses pulled up to the front of the school and began unloading. She wore a navy blue pantsuit and a festive holiday scarf. Green tree earrings dangled from her ears and a matching pin was on the front of her jacket. She easily towered over other teachers at 5'9 and her blue heels added to the height. In the mornings and afternoons, Anne was a dynamo, running up and down the tall staircases between the gym and cafeteria located on the bottom floor and the main office and entryway of the school as students streamed off busses.

As Principle of Fir Grove Elementary, she'd been voted Most Outstanding Principal on the North Coast for the last three years. Anne, along with her husband, Gavin Marks, who worked as Dean of Students and the high school basketball coach, were a dyno force. Moving to Cranberry Bay ten years ago after their son was injured by a drunk driver in Portland, and looking for a quieter place to settle, they'd easily slipped into the small-town community, bringing with them a passion and drive for education that benefited Cranberry Bay.

"Is your sister coming home for the holidays?" Anne asked Josh. She bit into a croissant and wiped powdered sugar off her lips. A few sprinkles still ended up on the front of her blue pantsuit and she quickly brushed them away. "Gavin is hoping she might be available to talk to some of the kids at the high school, do a little goal setting, motivation type thing."

"Suzanne will be home tonight," Josh nodded. "I'll let her know." Josh always looked forward to seeing his sister for the holidays. Ever since she'd taken the swim coach job at the University of Washington, her travel and competition schedule didn't allow her to return that often to Cranberry Bay. He glanced at the large white clock above the doorway. She'd be boarding her plane any minute. It was an hour flight to Portland, and then she'd rent a car and drive the ninety minutes over the Coast Range Mountains to Cranberry Bay. His parents always offered to pick her up but Suzanne always declined, not wanting to ask her older parents to take the drive, which sometimes in the winter could mean snow or ice on the mountain passes.

Ann's walkie-talkie burst into noise and a voice clipped, "Mrs. Marks. We need you down here in the gym."

"Have a great day," Anne said, smiling at Josh and Caitlin.

As she pushed open the door, a child banged on a door. "Mr. Morton! Mr. Morton!"

Josh gathered his mail from his box and hurried out the door toward his student. When he reached him, he knelt at eye level. "What's the matter, Alex? Why aren't you at breakfast with everyone else?"

"I don't want to go to breakfast," Alex clutched his backpack closer to him. "Connor is being mean to me."

"Come on in." Josh unlocked his door and ushered Alex inside. Connor teased Alex a lot the last couple days. Josh suspected it had something to do with the new brother who just joined Alex's home and he needed to feel like he was in control. But it didn't mean that Alex needed to start the day in tears. Josh strode to his desk, reached inside and grabbed a breakfast bar. He opened the small refrigerator next to his desk and pulled out a small carton of milk. "Here you go."

Josh made a small note on his clipboard and adjusted a couple of the laminated pieces of paper. They'd start with a class circle and a story this morning instead of the regular morning work time. He went to the class library and pulled out a picture book about three animal friends in the woods who learned to get along without bullying each other. He placed it on the big rocking chair along with the classroom stuffed alligator who always helped with circle time.

The voices of children's laughter bubbled down the hall. He stepped outside his classroom door and raised his finger to his lips to quiet them to an inside voice. Missy stepped forward and took her place as leader of the class. It was her job to lead the rest of the class down the hallway as they walked to recess, back to the classroom, and later to PE class. All of his students changed classroom jobs weekly in the morning meeting time. As his students came into the room, leaving coats and bags in the small cubby hooks outside in the hallways on the polished wood floors of the old school, he ushered them onto the carpet for story hour, each taking their specific places on the colorful squares of the large rug.

Josh felt lucky he was able to get the job from beloved teacher Allison Mahony when she retired. She'd been his supervising teacher and gave him most of her classroom supplies including the large carpet, a classroom library filled with decades of picture books, tubs of math manipulatives, and a closet full of old curriculum she hadn't the heart to throw away.

Josh added to the classroom's digital space, making sure each child owned a Chromebook through a grant he obtained for the school, storing the Chromebooks on a small cart in the back of the room, outfitting a center with musical CDs and earphones students could listen to, and creating a time-out area filled with a comfortable bean bag and stuffed bears in a darkened corner of the room.

He waved at Alex to come from the time-out corner and join them in the circle.

For the next twenty minutes, Josh led his class through listening to the story and passing the magic talking wand so each child could talk about how they felt listening to the story. He was pleased to hear Connor turn to Alex and apologize to him, and by the end of circle time, the two boys headed to the same math center to share manipulatives and work on their addition and subtraction.

The day passed quickly as the students moved through math centers, reading time, recess, and then off to their PE class.

"See you in thirty minutes." Josh waved to his class.

"Josh," Anne stopped him in the hallway. "I'm sorry to do this and I know this is your planning time, but Molly's daughter is sick and she needs to run up to the high school to pick her up. Can you cover her class? She said they are working on writing and it should be pretty easy for you."

"Sure," Josh ducked into his class and grabbed a stack of the morning work from his desk with a handful of stickers. Fifth graders were much more independent than second graders and it'd be easy to keep an eye on the class while he was catching up on getting things graded. One of his parent volunteers was coming this afternoon and it'd be great to have a stack of papers for her to slip into the student's take home folders sitting in the file box by the door.

Josh took the stairs two at a time until he reached the third floor of the school. Narrative essays and posters detailing the cycle of salmon decorated the hallways. He ducked into the third classroom on the left and set his papers on the desk. He held up his hand in the quiet signal for the noisy class.

After a minute, the class settled enough for him to be able to remind them of the rules for working.

Tyler raised his hand from his table group to the left

of the classroom door. "Mr. Morton. I have a question," he said without waiting to be called on.

Josh strolled to him. "Do you need some help?"

"It's about the Holiday Express," Tyler said.

Twenty-six pairs of eyes lifted their heads and faced Josh. Josh guessed that not one student in this room believed in Santa, but a part of them still hoped that maybe somewhere Santa was real, somehow.

"Do you need any elves?"

Josh tossed back his head and laughed as a chorus of voices shouted, "I want to be an elf."

"Yes," Josh said. "I do need some elves." He grinned, remembering his own days working as an elf on the Holiday Express. He was in fifth grade when he got his first assigned elf job. The elves played very important roles on the train trip to the North Pole. They helped pass out candy canes, sat with children who needed a little extra settling, and reassured children who were a little nervous about meeting Santa. When they reached the North Pole, elves made sure children got to see Santa and got back on the train when it was time.

"We can't choose all of you," he said. "What we'll need you to do is tell us why you would make the best elf. Practice the writing skills you are working on."

The fifth graders clicked into their Chromebooks and began furiously typing.

Josh chuckled and pulled up the stool at the front of the class and perched on it, sifting through the stack of papers and adding stickers to each one. When the bell rang to dismiss the fifth graders to lunch, the hum of voices in the classroom increased and Josh headed back down the stairs behind them to his own classroom. At his desk, he picked up his cell phone he'd left by his computer.

I've arrived, Suzanne texted fifteen minutes ago. *See you after school. Kami and I enjoyed lunch a few weeks ago. So excited to start helping her plan her wedding!*

It'd be good to have his sister back for the holidays. But Kami obviously hadn't said anything to Suzanne about their break. He drummed his fingers on the desk. Suzanne couldn't wait until the two of them would be sisters-in-law, she'd been talking about it since Kami first started dating Josh. He was going to need to tell her the truth. It wasn't going to be easy, but it was time to start telling people he and Kami were not going to be together.

Josh typed a Christmas tree and a small Santa emoji and hit send as a text from Ivy flashed across his screen. *Can you stop by and run another box of the plastic Santas to Mrs. Philips?*

Of course, Josh texted. He was glad his best friend, Keith, asked him to watch over Ivy this holiday season. The three of them had always been close, ever since Keith and Ivy moved to Cranberry Bay to live with their foster parents, who lived next door to him. They bonded over bike rides to the river in the summer and makeshift tents made of sheets and chairs, lying on sleeping bags and staring at the stars.

"Watch over Ivy," Keith said. "Just don't let her know you are doing it."

Josh agreed. He knew Ivy liked her independence and that she didn't want to need anyone. But everyone needed someone, especially during the holidays.

And, Josh's stomach nagged at him, the kiss he'd exchanged with Ivy on the Holiday Express all those years ago. He tried to push it away and tell himself it was just a high school boy's crush and nothing more. But after all the time with Kami, he never felt the same way he did about Ivy. There was nothing logical about it. He was sure she'd long forgotten, and he should, too.

Ivy's emoji smiley face lit up his screen and his heart.

Chapter 3

Ivy looped an evergreen garland to a hook above the red door to the antique shop. She stood on the top ladder rung and unhooked the Red Door Antique sign that hung above the door. Every year, she painted a new sign on a piece of plywood, changing the small items around the lettering. This year's sign she'd designed with the steam engine of the Holiday Express train in the left-hand corner and a set of train tracks following a sign that said, "To the North Pole."

She'd painted small white snowflakes as a border and swirling around the steam engine. Winters in Cranberry Bay seldom included snow. Usually, it was rain and heavy windstorms. But every year, the question always bubbled on everyone's lips, especially in the days leading up to Christmas, would they have a white Christmas?

"Careful, Ivy." Tom's voice boomed as he grabbed the ladder. "Everyone needs someone to hold the ladder." Tom, the owner of Cranberry Bay Hardware and

Lumber, stood beneath the ladder. He wore a flannel shirt, jeans, and work boots. His blue eyes sparkled in his round face and a grey beard.

"I'm just about finished." Ivy finished hanging the sign and tucked the garland into the last hook alongside the side. She climbed down the ladder and jumped off the last steps. "I underestimated how high that hook is for the sign." She placed the red plastic lid on the tub labeled front door and slid it beside a green one labeled, "Front Window."

"You shouldn't be doing this by yourself." Tom's eyes sparkled. "Next time, give me a call. I'm never too busy to help you keep up your legend as the Best Decorated Holiday Shop in Cranberry Bay."

Ivy smiled at Tom. Bright blue eyes peered out from a weatherworn face caused by years of fishing in all types of weather off the coast. Every Sunday, rain or shine, Tom was on his boat or selling his fish. He often supplied the food bank with fresh fish, and in the summer, set up a stand alongside the river cottages with a large sandwich board, Fish For Sale. Tourists traveling the coastal highway often stopped and lines could be seen all day on Sunday, snaking around the cottages as they waited eagerly for a chance to buy some of Tom's fish.

"I wouldn't pull you away from the hardware store. You don't have help right now, do you?"

Tom's Hardware, the only hardware shop in Cranberry Bay, had a bustling business that catered to locals and also Seashore Cove. Tom's Hardware sold everything from cleaning products to paper towels to nails and lumber. At one point, Tom tried to open a small restaurant with picnic tables in the summer and a couple tables and a bar in the winter. But it was too hard to find workers, and last year he'd closed it.

"Nah," Tom shook his head. "Can't get anyone to work these days. Cost of living has gone through the roof. Beach houses are swept up for rentals and investment property and the locals have nowhere to live. Used to be you could get a decent house in Cranberry Bay. Not anymore."

"I've got the same problem." Ivy reached into the large red box labeled Door, and pulled out another strand of thick garland. She slid three red bows from a small plastic bag and straightened the edges. The bows and garland were starting to look a little frayed, but they'd last another year before she replaced them. "I haven't been able to open the ice cream counter in the back of the store since late August when Cooper went back to college." Ivy looped one of the red bows over the door frame and attached two hooks at the bottom of the door. "How's your door decorating going?"

"Got it done." Tom grinned. A blast of wind blew around the corner of the building and Tom zipped up his red down jacket over his red flannel shirt. Every year, the merchants along Main Street tried to draw tourists into their shops by participating in a friendly door decorating contest. Large, colorfully decorated voting boxes sat on each counter of the stores participating in the door decorating contest. Anyone could vote on which one was the best.

Sasha usually enticed people to vote for her shop with a plate of freshly baked cookies beside her voting box. One year, Gracie, owner of the River Rock Inn, hired the local high school talent to play her piano in the front entryway of her boutique hotel and keep the holiday tunes going. The high school choir joined for the night of the judging, and she easily swept the first-place prize.

For the last three years, Ivy earned the first-place winner of the door decorating contest. Each year, she scoured eBay, searching for the perfect vintage model train car for Josh to gift his grandfather. She'd just been about to give up when a set flashed across her screen of a holiday model set. She'd hit her bid and watched the model set all week. No one outbid her and the train set became hers. It wasn't hard to find the lighted houses to place around the train. Once a collector's item, people got tired of setting up the villages each year and they languished in boxes in attics until someone brought them to Ivy and, with a pleading look, asked her to sell them. She walked around the vendor's booths and picked out six village houses including a Santa's workshop, library, school, and a tall Victorian home, and placed the tracks among the houses.

She painted small signs that said, Holiday Express and Santa's Workshop. Miniature people walked in her town and boarded the train bound for the Holiday Express. It was an instant hit with locals and tourists. She'd easily won the first-place prize and continued to win it as she added to the train set each year.

Tom only hung a couple red bows on the door to the

Hardware shop. "Don't want to compete with you, Gracie, Sasha, and Katie," he always said to Ivy.

"It feels so different on Main Street this year without Katie's sewing shop," Ivy pointed to the large storefront on the left side of the Red Door Antique shop. That summer, Katie closed her fabric shop and opened a new space in a large barn two miles outside of town on property which once belonged to her neighbor, Sawyer, a neighbor she despised. But all that changed when they'd fallen in love, gotten engaged, and merged neighboring properties. Now, Katie's fabric and sewing machine were happily nestled in a large red barn which Sawyer updated to include fir floors, a polished wood beam ceiling, and large glass windows that overlooked the sprawling farmland and valley. She planned to announce a slate of spring classes after the holiday season, including sewing classes for kids, quilting classes, and even an embroidery class which Gracie encouraged her to offer.

"Looks like Paige is getting into the spirit," Tom pointed to the red and green dog paws in the front window, each with a name and a donation amount given to the local animal shelter. A red bucket of dog treats hung from a nail outside the shop. In the front window, a petite blonde woman placed a black and white stuffed dog with a ribbon tied around his neck.

"Mmm...." Ivy gritted her teeth. Paige opened her shop four months ago in the space where Katie used to own her shop and a steady stream of people and dogs poured in. She offered basic dog obedience classes in the evenings in the back of the shop as well as a regular weekend event where the animal shelter brought a couple dogs to the store for a few hours so people could get to know them and fill out adoption applications. The town loved having a pet shop and Paige quickly expanded her shelves to include a wide variety of foods for both cats and dogs, bedding, toys, and a refrigerator filled with raw meat. On the other side of Paige's Pet Shop, Gracie started offering two pet friendly rooms on the ground level of her boutique hotel.

It wasn't bad having a bustling shop next to the Red Door Antique shop. But Paige also tried to take over the Cranberry Bay Business Association with her trendy ideas from Seattle. Every meeting, she presented a new idea which would increase tourism and business in Cranberry Bay. She wanted an annual dog festival with a dog show that would include all types of dogs and benefit the animal society. She wanted the shops to all coordinate for special sale days, something Ivy found challenging with her multiple vendors and their wants. And she wanted a vote for the animal of Cranberry Bay pretend mayor election. But the worst part was she wanted everything to be done immediately. Every new idea sent Ivy further into panic. She didn't mind trying new ideas, but she liked everything in her shop planned well in advance and all the angles and options considered. A long-standing member of the Chamber, Ivy took pride in her membership and responsibilities. Paige was proposing events and ideas with no time for implementation or planning. Ivy wished she would close her shop and go back to Seattle.

"Gracie's door is looking pretty good," Tom said.

Ivy peeked around the ladder toward Gracie's inn.

A large, colorful Christmas banner flew from a small post and two large pots with small evergreens framed the doorway. Each tree was decorated with twinkling white lights, and golden and silver ornaments hung from the limbs.

"I don't know," Ivy shook her head. "The first gust of wind that comes blasting through in a storm is going to knock all those ornaments to the ground."

Tom tossed back his head and laughed. "You are competitive, Ivy!" He pointed to her sign which hung by a thin rope above her head. A small gust of wind blew around the building and the sign twisted and turned, slipping off the hook and dangling at an angle. "You might want to secure your sign, too."

Ivy scurried back up the ladder. "Could you grab my hammer and another hook? Both of them are on the counter in the shop."

"Oh no you don't, Ivy," Tom said, placing his feet firmly on the ground around the ladder. "I'm not moving."

Ivy scurried down from the ladder. She nudged Tom playfully with her shoulder. "Stay right there."

When she stepped into the antique shop, white stuffing lay all over the shop floor.

"Max!" Ivy hollered for her dog. "Where are you?"

Ivy leaned down and picked up the remnants of a stuffed snowman. Six of the snowman's closest friends lay alongside him, each of their stuffing pulled out and tossed on the floor. Ivy didn't need to look at her clipboard. She knew who requested each specific item every year for the Holiday Homes Tour. The snowmen were always requested by Bill and Marianne Withers. They owned the 1925 Craftsman home that'd been in Bill's family for decades. Bill's parents and grandparents owned the house, and his grandmother loved snowmen. When Marianne volunteered for the home to be on the tour, she immediately came to Ivy and requested all the snowmen. This year, a woman donated an entire box of the snowmen, all handsewn.

But now those snowmen lay on the floor in tatters.

Max wagged his tail.

"Everything okay?" Tom's round face appeared in the door, and his mouth formed a large O.

He bent down and picked up a handful of the fluffy stuffing. "Looks like a few of your snowmen melted."

"With the help of one big dog who needs training." Ivy grabbed Max by the collar and hustled him under the counter. She placed a large treat on his dog bed. "Stay."

Max attacked the dog treat the same way he attacked the stuffing and then slipped from under the counter and headed back to the box of snowmen.

Ivy whisked the box out of the way and dropped it on the counter. "After Christmas we are going to dog training!" This afternoon, she vowed to go online and sign Max and her up for a dog training class in Seaside Cove. There was no doubt about it, Max needed training if she wanted to keep her sanity in the shop.

A cluster of women gathered with their dogs outside Paige's shop. "Come in," Paige called, her voice carrying through the open door of the Antique Shop. "Our morning training class is just about to start. Please walk your dogs to the back of the shop and practice 'leave it' as you go."

Ivy gritted her teeth as she clipped Max's leash to his collar and tethered him to one of the posts of the counter. She slid the bed toward him, and as she turned to head back outside, his howls filled the shop. She steeled her shoulders and hoped the class next door couldn't hear Max's whines.

Training needed to happen soon. But the last person she was going to ask for help was her rival next door.

Chapter 4

osh opened the back screen door and inhaled the Italian seasonings and garlic bread. His mom, Beth Morton, stood with her back to him, stirring a pan of spaghetti sauce. She straightened her frame and her dark hair swung on her shoulders. She wore a paisley skirt, black leggings, and a red sweater. Her feet were encased in a pair of fuzzy slippers. His sister, Suzanne, leaned against the counter. Tall and thin, Suzanne wore a red warm-up jacket, black yoga pants, and her feet were covered in fuzzy green socks. Her hair was pulled up in a scrunchy on top of her head.

"Smells wonderful," Josh said and dropped his arm around his mom's shoulder. "What can I do to help?"

Princess, a tabby cat with a white chest and sharp grey eyes, wound her way around his legs.

"Can you set the table?" Beth asked without taking her eyes off the bubbling pan.

"Sure thing," Josh walked to the cabinet and

opened it.

Suzanne nudged her hip against his. "Good to see you, little brother."

Josh embraced Suzanne in a hug. "Great to have you home for Christmas." He felt Suzanne's thin frame underneath her warm-up jacket and frowned. She hadn't mentioned anything about losing weight.

A shadow passed over Suzanne's face before she covered it with a bright smile. "I'm glad to be home." She picked up the *Cranberry Bay Gazette* from the small desk beside the kitchen counter. The back page listed the holiday events for the season. "Tree lighting, toy donation wrapping, soups for Santa, so much to do! I don't remember this many Christmas activities when we were younger."

"The Cranberry Bay Business Association has started a lot of new events over the last few years." Beth carried the pot of steaming sauce to a bowl to the table.

Josh smiled. Katie, Gracie, Ivy, and Rylee were masters at creating new events for Cranberry Bay. "The Fall Festival was started a couple years ago, and everyone wanted more activities throughout the year. The shops, hotels, and restaurants are all very happy with the new visitors."

"Grandpa drove the Fall Harvest Train," Suzanne said, her voice deepened. "I'm sorry I missed his Celebration of Life."

"I think he'd understand. He knew how important your swimming is to you," Josh said. "How is the team this year?"

Suzanne's swim team schedule conflicted with family events most of Josh's life. But it was a disappointment she hadn't been able to attend the Celebration of Life held in October. The Fall Harvest Festival had gone on, but the Harvest Train carrying people to a large pumpkin field remained parked along the small Cranberry Bay boarding platform. Ivy and Gracie decorated the station with festive fall wreaths and pumpkins. They placed two black ribbons alongside each of the platform's posts to honor Daniel Morton and his years of owning the Cranberry Bay steam engine.

Suzanne busied herself with folding cloth napkins. "The team didn't qualify for the holiday swim meets. I'm taking a little break from the team." She looked up and smiled brightly. "I hope I can get involved with some of these new Cranberry Bay Holiday events." Her smile didn't reach her eyes.

"Don't forget the Holiday Homes Tour," Beth said. "They can always use volunteers to docent in the homes."

"I'd love to be a docent," Suzanne said, but her voice sounded too bright. "We have beautiful historic homes."

Silence settled in the kitchen. Beth took the garlic bread from the oven. Josh pulled out four red and blue ceramic plates from the cabinet. The first holiday season without someone was always hard. Josh remembered when his grandmother passed away. He was in high school, and his grandfather spent most of Christmas Day sitting in a chair and staring at the tree, a sad look on his face. But this first year without Grandpa seemed much harder. The whole town was mourning his passing. And this year, driving the Holiday Express would be his job. A small pit in his stomach churned.

"I thought it might be fun to get involved with the Holiday Express this year." Suzanne's voice broke into his thoughts.

Josh swallowed hard. For as long as he could remember, Suzanne never wanted to help with the Holiday Express. Her swim season always fell during the winter holidays, and she'd been busy, traveling all over the state to compete. After she went to college, holiday visits were brief, forty-eight-hour events that fit around her college swim team meets. And then, she'd taken the job as swim coach at the University of Washington, rarely returning for the holidays at all as the swim season demanded her time over winter breaks. The Holiday Express was something his grandfather shared with him, something he kept close to him while his parents always seemed to be at Suzanne's swim meets.

"How about it?" Suzanne asked as she laid out the silverware alongside the plate. "Don't you think I'd look great as an elf?"

"You would be great as an elf." Josh cleared his throat. "But the fifth graders are going to be elves. We usually have a couple of the train board members who act as supervising elves."

Suzanne tucked a long strand of hair behind her ear. "How about Mrs. Claus?"

Josh shook his head. "Mrs. Claus is always reserved for Maureen." For as long as he could remember,

Maureen played Mrs. Claus while her husband, Tom, worked as Santa. Tom and Grandpa were best friends and, together, worked hard to bring the Holiday Express to life in the early days.

Suzanne took a step back. A hurt look flashed across her face.

"I'm sorry." Josh didn't want to dampen his sister's enthusiasm for the Holiday Express. "It's just…" he trailed off. "Tradition." It was tradition in Cranberry Bay to have the same people take the same roles on the Holiday Express. Cranberry Bay prided itself on things staying the same, no matter what.

"It's okay," Suzanne said, her voice filled with hurt. "I understand."

Josh grabbed a knife from the butcher block and sliced the bread with solid cuts. This year's change without his grandfather was going to be hard enough. the last thing he wanted to do was start making changes in everyone's roles on the train. But he couldn't exclude his sister. She was family.

"How about gift wrapping?" They always needed extra hands in the gift wrapping. Katie supervised the gift wrapping, and he'd check with her and see if they could add Suzanne.

"Sure," Suzanne said, her voice brightened. "That would be fun. Kami and I used to love to gift wrap. Do you remember the year when we color-coordinated every single present?"

"Sure do," Josh said and smiled, glad his sister seemed cheered up about the Holiday Express.

"Kami is so excited to come home," Suzanne said. "She said there is nothing like a Cranberry Bay Christmas."

Josh fiddled with the breadbasket. "About Kami—"

"Dinner's ready," Beth interrupted him and carried a bowl of fresh green salad to the table. "Can one of you tell your dad? He's been working on Daniel's trains all afternoon in the basement."

"Sure." Josh placed the bread on a platter and carried it to the table, grateful for the minute to take a deep breath and step out of the room. His relationship with his sister was never simple for him. It was one of the reasons why he loved spending time with Ivy and Keith. Their sibling relationship was effortless, and it'd been easy to pretend Ivy was his little sister, too, until he kissed her.

With Suzanne, it wasn't just her friendship with Kami. It took him a long time to find his own way, a way that didn't involve sports or athletics. His grandfather's strong presence guided him to a degree in teaching and reassured him that he did have his own path. It'd been hard to see how much time his parents spent with Suzanne at her swim meets, and his own school events and successes felt like they'd gone unnoticed. Josh headed toward the basement and the sound of the whoosh of granddad's trains as they whisked around the tracks.

⸻

AFTER DINNER, Josh parked alongside the single-story, brightly lit shingle siding library. The library was tucked behind the post office and across the street from The River Rock Inn. A single light glowed from the upper room of the inn. In the window, Gracie's head bent over a computer. The town was empty except for the River Tavern parking lot where three cars parked in front of the one-story building. Josh picked up his black, soft satchel and hopped out of the car. He took three steps to the heavy wood library door and opened it, making sure it closed firmly behind him.

Rebecca Shuster stepped out from behind the tall desk and computer at the front of the library. As the town's long-time librarian who recently retired, she still volunteered three days a week at the check-out desk and supervised some of the evening events. The town didn't have many meeting space options, and the library's main room was often booked for everything from Girl Scout Meetings to lecture series on the area's wildlife.

"Would you like to sit at the large table? I've started a fire and it should be warm soon." The library's heating system always seemed to be breaking, but the fireplace with the stone mantel filled the room with heat.

Josh nodded and smiled at her. "That would be great. It's a cold night and it'd be great to warm up."

Josh walked to the table and sat down on the far-left side. He never liked to take the head chair, even though after his grandfather died, he stepped into his new temporary role as President of the Cranberry Bay Historic Train Board, at least until the next board elections, which would happen in January.

The library door opened, and Tricia and Maureen

walked in together. Both women carried over-the-shoulder bags. Maureen set her bag down and went to the closet in the library where they kept the large coffee pot. Tricia pulled out a gold foil package with a shiny green tree.

"Holiday Blend." She waved the bag in the air. "Sasha's coffee has a new packaging this year."

"Did someone say holiday blend?" Adam Shuster strode from a plush red chair in the nature section of the library. He wore hiking boots, a fleece sweatshirt with the local park emblem, and heavy work jeans. "I've been clearing out the trail behind the library all afternoon and am chilled to the bone."

"Coming up." Maureen plugged in the coffee pot and filled it with water from the sink in the back storage room.

Adam pulled out a chair closest to the fire while Tricia sat down and pulled out stacks of papers and a small laptop computer from her bag.

"Sorry I'm late!" Ivy hurried into the library. She carried a white box with the bakery's gold seal. "Sasha sent these cookies along. She and Tyler have been baking all afternoon and wanted us to have the first taste at this year's holiday cookie."

She placed the box in the middle of the table with a stack of festive napkins and pulled out a chair next to Josh.

"The first taste of this year's holiday cookie!" Adam picked up a frosted reindeer. He bit into the cookie. "Nothing beats Sasha's gingerbread cookies."

"Shall we get started?" Josh opened his satchel and dug for the manila folder under the ungraded math papers. "I've got tonight's agenda." He handed out a single sheet of paper to each person seated at the table. The Cranberry Bay Historic Train Board always ran very informally. There were no calendar invites, no fancy slides, and no emailed agenda. His grandfather didn't believe in a lot of technology. *"Takes away from the Human connection,"* he always said. *"The important part is we have a team of people who believe in the train."*

But, in the last few months, the board quietly made some changes. Ivy stopped taking handwritten notes and typed them on her laptop. Tricia brought her laptop to go over the financials. Both women emailed copies to all the board members and requested any changes be noted before the meeting. But Josh hadn't the heart to email the agenda and continued to make copies on the school printer before the meeting.

"First order of business is the financials." Josh turned to Tricia.

Tricia was a fireball. Married to the town fire chief and a keen financial wizard, she volunteered as the treasurer for many of the non-profits in town.

"Everything is looking good," Tricia said. "We had a good fall harvest. The weather helped us out a lot. And people made donations. They wanted to honor Daniel."

Josh swallowed. Donations showed up not only at the Harvest Festival but also tucked into his mailbox at school.

"If we meet our projected earnings for the Holiday Homes Tour, we should finish the year in the black."

"Ticket sales are going well," Ivy said. "A steady stream of sales came in from the website and our promotions on social media are really drawing attention."

"How's the train running, Josh?" Maureen asked. "Anything you see that needs to be fixed?"

"I haven't looked her over since we housed her for the Fall Harvest. But I'm hoping to take a look this weekend." Josh scrawled a note to himself on his agenda.

Tricia noted a few more details about the budget and then closed her computer. "Let's talk about the Holiday Express." She pulled out a large butcher sheet of paper and unrolled it. Ivy stood and grabbed one end, and Tricia held the other. They attached it with blue painter's tape to the wall of the library.

A complex maze of colored lines and boxes filled the chart. Each detail of the Holiday Express's Christmas Eve route was outlined and laid out in intricate detail. Times were charted in ten- and fifteen-minute increments to show the route of the train as it made its' way to the pretend North Pole. Beside each box was another small circle with the names of the people who volunteered for each part of the route.

"What changes do we need to make this year?" Tricia asked. "We've got a different location for our North Pole, thanks to Sawyer's generous offer to use his land. It will make the route a little shorter, so we'll have to make some adjustments along the way."

"We've got a lot of names for the elves." Ivy pulled up

the spreadsheet which linked to the elf interest form on the website. Quietly, she'd modernized the train's roles in the last few years.

Josh flushed. "Sorry about that. I covered for the fifth-grade teacher today and students were excited about the elf jobs."

"It's okay," Ivy said, smiling at him. "I think we can use all of them this year. There will be lots of opportunities for helping with the hot cocoa when we get to the North Pole."

"And when we get to the North Pole," Tricia tapped the paper. "We'll have more time to visit with Santa."

"Katie is going to turn her barn into Santa's workshop," Ivy said. "We will have a covered walkway to Santa's Workshop and won't have to worry about the possibility of rain and kids getting wet."

The whole table breathed a collective sigh. All of them remembered more than one rainy Christmas Eve with shivering children and upset parents when the train arrived back at the station.

"Good," Josh nodded. "What other changes do we need to make?"

Maureen cleared her throat. "We're going to need a Santa and Mrs. Claus. Tom and I are going to be visiting our first grandchild in Seattle. Our daughter is due any day!"

"Congratulations!" Tricia and Adam said at the same time.

Josh exhaled. He was happy for Tom and Maureen, but they'd played Mr. and Mrs. Claus for as long as he could remember. Longtime friends of his grandfather, the three of them enjoyed the festive train ride and spent weeks discussing each moment of the night.

"Congratulations!" Josh tapped his pencil on the table. "It looks like we need a Santa and Mrs. Claus." He gazed across the room at Ellen Shuster, who ducked her head and stared very hard at the computer screen.

"Rebecca? You'd make a great Mrs. Claus. We could ask Mayor Mays if he'd play Santa."

Rebecca raised her head and shook her head. Her cheeks flushed. "I don't think I'm up for that role. Christmas can be pretty busy around the Shuster house, especially with Sawyer and Bryan adding to our family the last couple years."

Maureen shook her head. "I think Mayor Mays is going to be pretty busy with his twins. They were in Tom's Hardware looking at decorations and he couldn't keep them from pulling anything they could from the shelves."

"What about you, Josh?" Adam asked.

"Me?" Josh asked.

"With the new location, there would be time for you to get into Santa's suit."

"He's right," Maureen said. "Your grandfather never could play Santa because of the timing of the stop at the North Pole. He and Tom often discussed how they could change the route so he could play Santa, but it wasn't possible until Sawyer offered his land as the North Pole."

Josh loved driving the train. He swallowed and felt the weight of the world on his shoulders. The entire town depended on the Holiday Train tradition for their Christmas Eve. Churches even scheduled their Christmas Eve services at four p.m. to allow time for the children to board the Holiday Express train in their pajamas at seven.

"You can do this," Ivy touched his arm. "You always loved the Holiday Express. Taking on the role of Santa is just one more way to show how much you love this tradition. It's a part of who you are."

Josh gazed around the table at the people who'd been through the ups and downs of the historic train. They'd worked through seasons where it seemed they'd never sell enough tickets to cover the operating costs. They committed their time each holiday season to the train and again throughout the year as they met as a board to discuss budgets and repairs. And Ivy was one of those people. For years, she played the role of head elf on the train, guiding the children to their seats, making sure they were happy and enjoying the ride, and then guiding them off to Santa. It was time she played a bigger role on the train.

Josh turned to Ivy. "I want you to be Mrs. Claus."

Ivy's face paled. "Me? Mrs. Claus?"

"Yes," Josh said, assurance filling his voice. "We can do this together." He would be nervous filling the shoes of his grandfather, driving the train, and playing Santa, but with Ivy's calm and steady reassurance by his side, he knew he could do it.

Chapter 5

The next afternoon, Ivy pulled open the heavy doors to Katie's refurbished barn. A red sign hung above the door, proclaiming, "Santa's Workshop." The smell of cinnamon and woodsmoke filled the air. Sewing machines sat on long wood tables, and various colors of fleece fabric lay across the tables. Deep blue and red throw rugs covered the dark, refurbished wood floors. Large picture windows overlooked a rolling field of grass. A gas fire stove blazed the back left corner of the room.

"Sorry I'm late. I received another order for a box of vintage ornaments from the online shop and the post office line was out the door."

Ivy placed the 1970s Singer sewing machine on the table beside two new machines. She'd used the machine since high school when she found it at her foster mother, Carol's *Treasures and Trash* shop, tucked alongside a bucket of old glass fishing floats and a wood dresser with deep scratches in the sides. She fixed the needle so it moved smoothly over fabric and the bobbin wound without glitching. Ivy taught herself to sew, spending hours watching instructional videos and scrounging through the thrift store for clothing that needed a little mending. By the time she was a junior, other students were requesting her special clothing and bringing her thrift store finds to make into new creations for them.

Katie lifted her head from cutting pajama bottom pants on a huge cutting mat. "We're just getting started."

"I don't know why we didn't start this project in September," Rylee grumbled, biting into a large cream cheese Danish.

"Because," Gracie said from the plush chair by the fireplace where she nursed a cup of tea. "We were working on Halloween costumes for the children's parade."

Sasha wiped a rag over the counter beside a plate of croissants and fruit Danishes. "In October, we were sewing aprons for the Thanksgiving harvest festival."

Katie shook her head. "Well, maybe we should have Christmas in July." She swiped her rolling cutter through red fleece with festive Santa faces on it.

"Bags," Gracie said. "We were sewing bags for the summer market and July 4th Festival."

"Maybe we went a little overboard with festivals for Cranberry Bay." Katie placed the cut fabric on the growing pile of pajama pants to be sewn.

"The festivals have brought so much life to the town, and the Cranberry Bay Business Association is counting on the first spring festival this year." Sasha picked up a Cherry Danish. She bit into it and swallowed. "Not too bad."

"Not too bad?" Rylee said. "Sasha, these are amazing."

Ivy took a stack of the cut fabric and sat down in the chair behind a sewing machine. She quickly spooled a bobbin in the same deep cranberry red as the fabric and threaded the sewing machine needle.

A gust of wind blew the doors open. Lisa Sawyer and her sixteen-year-old daughter, Maddie, stepped inside, each carrying tote bags filled with fleece material.

"I think we bought out the store." Maddie dropped the heavy denim tote on the table. She rubbed her shoulder.

"Not even close." Lisa set her bag beside Maddie and smiled at her daughter. "I think there was at least one bolt with a bit of selvage."

"The best part of the trip to Seaview Cove was I got to drive."

Ivy glanced up from her sewing machine. "You got your license. Congratulations!"

Maddie reached into a small over-the-shoulder purse and pulled out a small piece of paper. "I am official now. Mom doesn't want me to drive in the dark. But living this far out from Cranberry Bay, I will get a lot of chances to run errands!"

Lisa and Maddie lived in the small carriage house separated from the big home where Katie lived with Sawyer and his ten-year-old daughter. A year ago, Lisa and Maddie returned to Cranberry Bay, and neither one of them was willing to talk about Maddie's trouble. It'd been a hard couple months for Maddie as she readjusted to the cozy town and the small high school where everyone looked out for each other. But in the last six months, she relaxed. Her clothing changed from all black outfits to colorful tops and denim jeans. She asked Lisa to take her to Sally and recolor her hair to her original blonde from the purple and blue colors which streaked through the long strands. She wore her hair pulled back in a red cloth hair band and her bright blue eyes shone from her clear complexion.

"You just need to pay for your part of the car insurance." Lisa tapped her daughter's shoulder and sat down beside the large stack of fabric.

"I could use some help at the shop," Ivy said. "It gets so busy at this time of the year with the online orders. I need someone to run to the post office and drop off the orders."

"That sounds perfect!" Maddie hopped up and threw her arms around Ivy. "I could use your car, right Mom?" Maddie turned to face Lisa, her best good girl look on her face which caused Sasha and Rylee to duck behind their sewing machines and cover their hands with their mouths to hide the smiles.

"I don't know." Lisa drummed her fingers on the table.

"You don't need the car," Maddie said. "You're taking all those online business classes, and if you need to run some errands, I could either do them for you or pick you up and drive you."

Lisa leaned back and crossed her hands over her chest. "How can I resist this offer? My own personal driver." She turned to Ivy. "As long as Maddie is not driving over to Seashore Cove in the dark, I don't have a problem with giving her my car to use for errands around Cranberry Bay."

"It won't all be driving," Ivy said to Maddie. "I need help in the shop, too. I haven't been able to open the ice cream counter since August and even though it's cold and rainy, there are still people in Cranberry Bay who love to stop in and get a scoop of ice cream."

"I would be happy to help with the ice cream counter," Maddie said. "I love ice cream."

"Perfect," Ivy nodded. "Stop by tomorrow after school and I'll show you around and help you get familiar with the different vendors and each area of the store."

"How is the funding this year for the train?" Rylee asked Ivy.

"The same," Ivy said. Every year, it was always down to the last minute as to whether the train would have enough funding to run the Holiday Express. The train operated on a shoestring budget, and although the summer and fall harvest runs brought in a chunk of their operating expenses, the Holiday Express depended on the Holiday Homes Tour tickets to bring in the revenue needed for the train to run on Christmas Eve.

"Sawyer has been chopping wood for days for the

bonfire," Katie said. "He's so excited to have the North Pole up here this year."

"He really saved the day when he stepped in and offered to have it here." Ivy slipped a piece of fleece under her machine needle and made sure to align the edges with the small, ruled lines alongside the needle.

"If that new mall hadn't been built on the old Wilkerson property," Sasha said, "we wouldn't have to relocate."

Katie ducked her head, and Rylee became occupied with threading her needle.

Ivy smiled. Katie and Rylee both fell in love with men who wanted to see progress and change brought to Cranberry Bay. Bryan Shuster's real estate office supported his older brother Sawyer with investing in land that offered large complex retail shopping and some small office buildings. Both were hoping to draw more work opportunities as well as more visitors to the small town.

"I forgot to tell you!" Katie stopped cutting and walked over to the plush chair by the gas fireplace. "Mom dropped off this basket of holiday children's books. Mrs. Claus is going to read to the children *The Night Before Christmas!*"

"That's a great idea!" Rylee grabbed three pairs of pant legs and sat down at the new sewing machine beside Ivy. "I loved holiday stories as a child. My favorite was *Father Christmas.*"

"I remember that one!" Sasha said, snapping her fingers. "The grumpy Santa Claus!"

"We have more time this year because the train isn't

going as far to the North Pole," Katie said. "You know she is always trying to encourage reading!"

"Maureen will be perfect reading to the children!" Gracie said. "She has such a nice voice, and she often reads to the children's story hour at the library."

Ivy pressed down hard on the foot pedal and guided the needle down the left side of the pant leg, sewing the two pieces of fabric together. She bit her lower lip. Maureen wasn't going to play Mrs. Claus. Josh asked her. And unlike her friends, who were so excited about holiday books, she did not have happy memories of reading holiday stories. Not only did she not have happy memories of reading holiday stories, she didn't have any happy memories of reading, period.

Sasha bent her head and pushed the fabric through the machine. "I talked to Tom this morning when he came in for his coffee. He's going with Maureen to see his new granddaughter."

"Who will play Santa and Mrs. Claus?" Gracie asked.

"Josh," Ivy said without lifting her eyes from her machine. "The train route is shortened this year, so he will have enough time to change into the Santa suit after driving the train."

"And who is going to be Mrs. Claus?" Sasha said. "Everyone has their roles for the Holiday Train."

Ivy's heart pounded. She couldn't form the words to tell her friends that Josh asked her to play Mrs. Claus. How could she play Mrs. Claus and read aloud to the children? For years, she kept it a secret that she struggled with reading. Math always came easily to her, and she'd excelled in all her math classes. But reading was a different story. She borrowed audiobooks and relied on text-to-speech to deceiver emails and documents. Moving around from school to school hadn't helped as she was shuffled around in reading groups. By the time she reached middle school, she learned to find the easy sections of the library, the books with pictures and large prints and few words on a page. She managed to score C's on most of her projects and tests with the help of her brother completing some of the work for her. In high school, the reading increased, and it was harder, but Keith always came to her rescue, providing her with his old tests and showing her how to find audiobooks. But Keith wasn't here to help her this time.

The chatter swirled around her as the women discussed who could play Mrs. Claus.

Ivy's heart pounded. Playing Mrs. Claus was no different than all the other times she and Josh worked together on volunteer projects for Cranberry Bay. The Holiday Express was the town's signature event. People carried the memories of their childhood Christmas Eve riding the Holiday Express and getting a toy from Santa all their lives. For all the boxes of antiques and old items people didn't want when they cleaned out Cranberry Bay homes, very rarely were the toys of the Holiday Express with their special gold train sticker on the back with the year ever found in the boxes.

Sasha tapped her arm. "Everything okay?"

"Of course," Ivy slipped the red fabric into the sewing machine and pressed hard on the pedal. She would figure out a way to get help with her reading and make sure that Josh's first year as the train conductor and Santa was a success. He was her friend and that's what friends did for each other. She pushed aside all other feelings about him that bubbled inside her. She would never risk that friendship. It was much better to maintain the status quo than gamble with her heart. As long as she didn't admit there was anything more than friendship, she could keep herself safe, safe from the possibility of loving someone and losing them, like her mom.

Chapter 6

J osh tossed the basketball into the net bag, hoisted it over his shoulder and walked to the gym closet. Kids streamed out of the gym toward parents waiting in the doorways and sitting on the bleachers. Afterschool basketball club always drew a crowd of parent spectators, especially in the dark winter evenings.

A thin boy with curly dark hair stood under the basketball hoop. "Just one more basket, Mr. Morton." He jumped up and pretended to slam a ball into the net. "You looked like Santa with the bag!"

"Your team did great, Mason," Josh grabbed the ball and tossed it into the net above his head. "What did you ask Santa for this year?"

"Nothing," Mason scuffed his foot on the floor. "I don't believe in Santa. I'm too old for that now."

"Everyone believes in Santa." Josh picked up the ball and placed it against his left hip. He tried to encourage the older elementary kids to keep their belief in Santa. It helped stop the younger ones from overhearing how parents were Santa. But more importantly, believing in Santa was the magic of Christmas. The idea that if you believed, the magic could happen.

"My dad says there's no Santa and believing in him is just foolish hope."

"Mmmm…" Josh clutched the ball to his side a little tighter. Mason's dad was sentenced to three years in prison six months ago. Mason had just gone to his first visitation. Josh didn't want to discourage Mason's relationship with his dad, but it didn't seem right to take away the hope of the magic of Christmas and Santa either. "Are you riding the Holiday Express this year?"

"Nah," Mason looked at the ground. "Mom says I'm too old. And if there's no Santa, it's stupid to go to the North Pole."

"I see," Josh studied the little boy. He wore a flannel shirt, dark denim jeans, and tennis shoes. "Would you like to be an elf on the train?"

"An elf?" Mason looked up at him, his eyes glowed with hope.

"Yep," Josh said. "We still need a couple more." They didn't need any more elves according to Ivy's spreadsheet from the sign-up form, but no one needed to know. He'd make sure to add Mason's name to the elf list tonight.

"Do I get to wear a costume?" Mason asked.

"You sure do!" Josh said.

"Whoo-hoo!" Mason jumped up in the air and high fived Josh. "I love costumes."

Josh looked around the empty gymnasium. "Who is picking you up tonight?"

"No one," Mason didn't look at Josh. "Mom's sleeping. I'm not supposed to bother her."

"Come on." Josh picked up his bag and slipped into his heavy down jacket. He pulled a knit cap on his head. "I'll give you a ride home."

Josh motioned toward Mike, who picked up a stray basketball beside the bleachers. "I'm heading out. Going to give Mason a ride home."

Mike waved at him. "Thanks for helping out!"

Josh nodded. He often pitched in to help with the afterschool basketball club. In the spring, Josh supervised the spring play production, and Mike often helped build the sets. When Anne took over as Principal, she emphasized keeping the kids involved after school. "Too many go home and sit in front of screens," she said. "I want them here and interacting with each other and I don't mean study clubs." Clubs sprung up in every corner of the school, art club, games club, creative writing club, and numerous sports ranging from volleyball to basketball. Caitlin won a grant from a bike shop to buy bikes and sponsored the bike club.

Josh motioned Mason toward the back door of the gym which led to the staff parking lot. Josh often gave Mason a ride home after clubs. During the summer, he taught driver's education at the high school and kept a driver's license which allowed him to transport students. Mason's mom worked the night shift at the local supermarket in Seashore Cove and his older sister was on the high school volleyball team. If the team was at an away game, there was no one to pick up Mason.

Josh tossed his satchel into the backseat of his car and Mason climbed into the passenger seat. He buckled the seat belt across his chest and sniffed. "I smell hamburger!"

Josh smiled. Mason always smelled food in his car. It was his hint that he wanted Josh to stop and get him a hamburger, fries, and a shake.

"I think I saw hamburgers on the lunch menu today." Josh pulled out of the staff parking lot. Mason lived in one of the apartments tucked behind the businesses of Cranberry Bay. The apartments were single-story, attached units designed to be simple apartments for families who needed assistance. Most of the units fell into some sort of disarray and needed everything from plumbing to electrical. A couple of the volunteer firefighters tried to keep an eye on the building and make sure the gutters were cleaned, leaks fixed, and when needed, hired a plumber or an electrician to look at a leak or detached kitchen wire.

"It's cold." Mason wrapped his arms around himself.

"Heat will be up in a minute." Josh flipped the heat switch to high. The winter temperature always hovered around forty degrees with a lot of rain. The dampness seeped into the buildings, cars, and crevices of every pocket of Cranberry Bay. Mason wore a thin raincoat. He made a mental note to check the clothing closet at school for a heavier coat to give to Mason.

Usually, Principal Marks made the school's donated

clothing closet available to Mason as she noticed outgrown pants or shirts. He wasn't the only student who Anne kept under her wing, quietly providing for them what they did not have. When the clothing closet got too low on a popular item, such as coats or boots, Anne often took a day to head to Portland and restock the clothing closet. It was one of the many things which made Anne so loved by the Fir Pines Elementary school staff.

Josh pulled up alongside the apartment units. A small lamp glowed in the window of one of the front units.

"Tammy is home!" Mason grabbed at the door handle. "Thanks for the ride, Mr. Morton!"

Mason hopped out of the car. The front door opened and a tall, slender teen wearing a warm-up jacket and sweats in the high school's colors embraced Mason.

She waved at Josh, and he honked his horn and pulled away from the curb. Josh turned the car and headed toward Main Street. Holiday lights glittered along the top of the buildings. In front of Paige's shop, lights in the shape of paw prints glowed a flashing red and green. Lights blazed from Ivy's shop windows and the open sign still hung on the door.

Josh parked the car alongside the antique shop and got out. He stopped and admired the front window. A black steam engine pulled a pullman car, two box cars and a small open flat car with a tall giraffe sticking its head out of the open top. A red caboose brought up the rear. The train wound its way past small lighted homes, over bridges and around the two-rail tracks. A small puff of steam came out of the steam car every time it passed by the double-crossing gate and the plastic people figures standing on the other side.

Josh pulled open the door and stepped inside the warm shop. Ivy worked at the front counter, her fingers moving quickly as she packaged a box filled with delicate Santa ornaments.

"Want me to flip the sign to closed? It's after five."

Ivy looked up at him, her eyes wide in panic. Max jumped to an alert stance and barked.

"Sorry! I didn't mean to startle you." Josh grabbed one of the treats in the blue dog basket on the counter. Max took the treat in one gulp, his teeth touching Josh's palm. Josh jerked his hand back.

"We need to work on a few things." Ivy grabbed Max's collar and dragged him away from Josh. "Sorry about that."

"I was on my way home after dropping Mason off and I saw your lights still on. I thought I'd see if you needed any help." Josh leaned against the counter. Ivy's cheeks flushed red. The clipboard by her side showed a neat row of checks and items crossed off. "Santa is working on her list." Josh pointed to the list and grinned. Christmas was not a joyful, spontaneous event for Ivy. It was a series of lists and tasks to be accomplished. He knew this year would be hard with Keith away, but he wanted to change the season for her, give her a holiday that was joyful and filled with the magic spark of the season.

Ivy pushed the hair away from her forehead. "I was just wrapping up." She grabbed a pen from a small jelly jar. "I want to have these ready to go tomorrow. I hired Maddie to help with the errands and work the ice cream counter on the weekend for the rest of the month. But there is still so much to do."

Max's tail thumped against the counter.

"Looks like someone is ready to go for his walk."

Max's tail thumped harder, and he whined.

"I give up." Ivy slipped the leash from the small hook behind her. "Let's go for a walk."

Josh grinned. "Everyone loves a walk."

Ivy grabbed her coat and Josh took it from her. He held it out and she turned around and stuck one arm in and then the other. Josh pulled the coat up around her shoulders. He breathed in the soft scent of lavender. For a minute, he couldn't move. His hands rested on Ivy's shoulders, transfixed by her.

The sharp bark from Max jerked Josh out of his thoughts. He squeezed Ivy's shoulders and stepped away.

When she turned to him, her cheeks were flushed. But she didn't say anything about the moment which just occurred between them. "Ready?"

"Always!" Josh followed her to the door and stopped at the front picture window. A model train whooshed as it ran by them on a track. Ivy leaned into the window to turn off the train.

"Wait," Josh laid his hand on top of Ivy's. "The animal flatbed car. Is it new?"

"Yes." Ivy turned to him, and her eyes sparkled. "I found it this summer online. The giraffe was missing, but

I was able to use one of the small animals from Beth's vendor booth.

"My grandpa owned a car like this one," Josh said. "We got it together at a train meet-up in Portland when I was twelve." His voice faded as the memories rushed back. There was always an auction with collector item train cars. His grandfather bought a couple tickets and never won. But that year, Josh saved money from his lawn mowing business. He bought five tickets and one of his tickets was drawn in the auction. Josh won the animal car.

"Do you still have it?" Ivy asked.

Josh nodded. "It's somewhere in the boxes." Josh swallowed. He was supposed to be helping his dad pack up some of his grandfather's many train sets. But he didn't have the heart to do it. His dad didn't seem to be making much progress, and every time Josh went into the basement, more cars and tracks appeared out of the boxes and not in them.

Ivy touched Josh's hand. "I know how hard this is," she said. "Losing your grandpa is like losing a part of you."

Josh nodded. The lump formed in his throat. "It's hard this year, Christmas, the train, without him." He swallowed.

Max pressed against Josh's leg as if he knew Josh needed comfort. Josh leaned down and petted the dog's soft fur. "That's enough of me," he straightened. "Someone needs a walk."

Ivy turned off the shop lights and flipped the sign to

closed but she didn't turn off the train and kept the picture window light on.

Josh stepped outside and inhaled the scent of the night, the river, and the evergreen trees which surrounded the town. White, red, and green lights twinkled along the roof line of the downtown businesses of Cranberry Bay. In the town park, the tall evergreen, which would become the town's Christmas tree, stood dark. Every year, Josh worked with Adam and a couple of the guys at Public Works to hang the lights a few days before the tree lighting. The lights formed a triangle all the way down the tree and a large star perched on top. This year's star was new and ordered from a company in New York. It just arrived and Josh dropped it off at the Public Works office this morning.

Josh placed his hand on the small of Ivy's back and steered her away from the antique shop. "Look at the lights." Josh pointed to the boardwalk leading to the river dock.

Small twinkle lights hung along the edges of the walkway. Two lighted deer, a mother and her fawn, stood at the beginning of the walkway.

"Rylee and Bryan decorated the walkway." Ivy pointed to the River Cottages beside the boardwalk, each decorated with colorful lights. A small sign and large plastic lighted Santa stood outside each cottage. Rylee scoured thrift shops all year for six large plastic Santas. She begged Ivy to tell her as soon as a plastic Santa showed up in someone's donation box. The last one arrived only days ago. Rylee rushed over and with the help of Bryan, carried it back to their cottages. Bryan grumbled to Josh about Rylee's Santa hunts, but Josh knew Bryan would do anything for Rylee, his former high school sweetheart.

Josh peered at Ivy, walking beside him. She held onto Max's leash, and her hands were encased in red mittens with a small strand of white fur along the edges. A matching hat with a small pom top sat on her head. A red and white scarf wrapped around her neck. The feelings for Ivy never changed from that moment of their kiss in high school. They still bubbled underneath the surface of his heart, making him feel joyful and hopeful and energetic.

When they got to the end of the boardwalk, Josh stood and looked out at the dark river. "Thanks for agreeing to be Mrs. Claus," he said, his voice soft. "I was really thrown when Maureen said she and Tom weren't going to be a part of the Holiday Express."

Ivy tensed and pulled Max's leash.

"You are okay with playing Mrs. Claus, right? You know you can tell me if you don't want to."

"I will play Mrs. Claus." Ivy didn't look at him, her voice clipped and brisk.

Josh exhaled. He was surprised at how much it meant to him that Ivy play Mrs. Claus, but he knew he didn't want anyone else with him in that role.

"The town doesn't like change, Josh," Ivy said. "They need to know that the train is carrying on the tradition of Cranberry Bay Christmas. That is why I will play Mrs.

MINDY HARDWICK

Claus. People are used to seeing me as a part of the Holiday Express."

Josh felt his heart drop. He hoped that Ivy was playing Mrs. Claus because he asked her, and she was doing it for him. It was a silly hope, really. Ivy was practical. She didn't hold onto foolish high school hopes like him. Ivy agreed to play Mrs. Claus because the Holiday Express was an important part of Cranberry Bay's Holiday Festivities. Ivy didn't believe in Santa and magic any more than Mason. He was grateful she'd agreed to play Mrs. Claus with all her other responsibilities this Christmas. "How are the lazy pants coming along?"

Ivy laughed. "Chaotic. We have piles to do, but," she touched his arm, "we'll get it done."

"Yes," Josh said. "I know you will. The five of you are amazing at everything you do for Cranberry Bay."

"We enjoy it," Ivy said. She turned to Josh. "Are you enjoying getting ready for the Holiday Express?"

Josh turned to her, a puzzled look on his face. "Of course. What do you mean?"

"I don't know," Ivy said. "It just seems something about you is different this year."

Josh exhaled loudly. Ivy always knew how to read him. The Christmas season did seem different this year. Suzanne was home and there was the unspoken expectation that an engagement announcement would be coming between him and Kami, something that he needed to tell everyone wasn't going to happen. And then there was the Holiday Express and carrying on his grandfather's train tradition. "You're right. I feel a lot of pressure with the Holiday Express. The town expects it to be the same every year, and this year it just doesn't feel the same."

"Your grandfather would have wanted you to drive the steam engine."

"I know," Josh said. "But with Grandpa gone and now Tom and Maureen and the North Pole is at a different place and the schedule is going to be different. It just feels like we are setting ourselves up to let people down."

"I understand," Ivy said, staring out at the river. "As a child, Christmas was often a disappointment. We were given gifts that people donated, but it never really gave me what I really wanted…"

Josh turned to look at Ivy. "What did you really want?"

"A family," Ivy said quietly. "When I first moved to Cranberry Bay to live with Carol and Rick, I used to love to take walks just at sunset. People hadn't shut their blinds yet and I could see inside the homes decorated for Christmas with the families eating dinner and sitting in the living rooms."

Josh wondered if Ivy walked by his house. Did she look inside and think about how nice their family looked? But not know how empty it was with Suzanne busy at swim meets, his parents coming home late after attending the swim meets, and his grandmother's two-year battle with cancer.

"It's why I always sponsor the Holiday Homes Tour," Ivy said. "It's that part of me who wants the perfect family Christmas. I like to create that image for others."

"I'm sorry, Ivy," Josh placed his hand on her lower back. "And Keith isn't coming home this year."

"It will be the first Christmas we are apart. We've always spent Christmas together," Ivy's voice softened. "Keith always made me something for Christmas. One year, it was a sign made of driftwood and stones. One year it was a stool for my sewing table." She breathed softly. "I miss him in Cranberry Bay. Not just at Christmas but all year."

"Why don't you come to Christmas brunch at my house?" Josh asked. "Mom is baking her cranberry bread and Dad is cooking a ham. I am going to do some sides and Suzanne will bake a pie." He turned to face Ivy. He didn't know why he hadn't thought of it sooner. Ivy couldn't spend Christmas alone. Katie and Rylee would be celebrating at the Shuster family's big holiday festivities, and Gracie always went to her sister's home in Seashore Cove.

"I don't know," Ivy said, her words halted. "I might just spend the day with the dog, take some walks, get some quiet time. A day to myself is nice." Her voice trailed off.

Josh peered into her eyes, searching.

But before he could say anything, a loud splash at the end of the dock jerked his attention away.

"Raisin!" Bryan's voice slashed through the night.

Raisin swam toward the festive lights on the board-walk. His form glowed in the water.

"I've got him," Josh reached into the cold waters, and when Raisin reached his hand, he grabbed the dog's collar and pulled him alongside the edge of the walkway and to the sandy shore. Raisin shook himself and water cascaded all around him and onto Josh.

"Thanks!" Bryan jogged up to Josh and clasped Raisin's leash to him. "What are you two doing out here?"

"We were viewing the lights," Ivy said. "They look great! You and Rylee really livened up this part of Cranberry Bay with the lights on all the cottages."

"It was a lot of work, but it did come out well." Bryan stood back and admired the lights twinkling from each of the cottages.

Raisin pulled on his leash and barked at Max.

"We'll see you at the tree lighting tomorrow night," Bryan said and allowed Raisin to pull him toward the cottages.

"I better go," Ivy said. "I still have some work to finish tonight."

"Let's go," Josh touched her elbow and steered her toward the lighted downtown Main Street and her store, neither of them mentioning the offer on the table for Christmas.

Chapter 7

A car honked outside the antique shop and rain slid down the shop's windows. Ivy clenched her jaw as a large SUV maneuvered for a spot in front of Paige's dog shop. All morning, people fought over the parking spots as they brought pets in for Paws for a Cause, photos with Santa. Ivy tried to remain upbeat and positive. People paid twenty dollars for a photo with Santa and their pet. The photos were printed and sent as a digital photo in an email. All Paws for a Cause donations were going toward the animal shelter in Seaview Shores. But it was hard to remain festive and cheerful when her own shop's foot traffic slowed to nothing.

The front door opened and the sleigh bells hanging from the door handle clunked together.

"It's busy out there." Abby Wilson wiped rain off her navy blue trench coat. "I am glad Bob dropped me off. The rain is really coming down."

Ivy smiled at one of her favorite vendors. "Your space is selling well. Everyone likes the vintage holiday cards."

"Those were a find," Abby said. "We just happened to stop off at an estate sale and there were boxes of cards. I've got Valentine's ones, too."

"The customers will love those." A car blared its horn outside. The customers were not loving Main Street parking. Each shop was assigned designated parking spaces. There were two for each business's employees and the rest were open on a first come, first served. Usually, it wasn't a problem. Even in the summer, the spots in front of the Main Street shops didn't fill, not like the surrounding beach towns. It was one of the areas the Cranberry Bay Business Association worked on, attracting more customers. But this wasn't what Ivy envisioned when Paige suggested a Paws for the Cause event. Ivy wrote herself a note on a sticky to talk to the Cranberry Bay Business Association about events at Paige's shop needing extra traffic control and designated spaces in the lot behind the post office. She was sure Paige could afford a few extra hours of Cranberry Bay's police time.

Abby placed her hands on the counter and leaned close to Ivy. "The vendors aren't happy this year with sales."

Ivy steeled herself for what she knew was coming. The vendors hadn't been happy all year. It wasn't just the Christmas sales. None of the year's sales were as brisk as in past years. Ivy tried to educate the vendors on prices and how they needed to stay competitive. But so many insisted on raising their prices, not lowering them. The vendors complained their costs increased and they couldn't sell things at rock bottom prices. Ivy tried to convince the vendors to host sales, but most of them only discounted ten percent which wasn't enough to entice a buyer. Ivy looked toward Paige's shop and the wall they shared. Laughter and dogs barking floated through the shared wall. Paws with a Cause lured people into Paige's shop. And who could resist a new dog toy, treats, or a bag of food?

"Maybe we should do a store-wide event?" Abby said. "Something like what Paige is doing. Something to draw in customers."

"We have the Holiday Homes tour," Ivy said. "That is the holiday event which is supposed to pull in revenue. But it wasn't so far. The Holiday Home ticket sales were coming from online, not from people walking into the store and buying tickets while purchasing a few gifts for their home."

"There's a new antique market opening in Seashore Cove," Abby said. "There's some talk a few of the vendors may leave…"

She broke off as the front door opened and Maddie flew into the store, her cheeks flushed pink and breathless. She wore a heavy down jacket and a festive red plaid skirt with long black tights and black boots. A black knit cap perched on her head and her blonde hair tumbled around her shoulders.

"Ivy," Maddie said. "I'm so sorry, but Paige needs extra help today. Is it okay if I help out? It's just for today.

And," she glanced around the shop, "it's not very busy in here."

Ivy couldn't argue with Maddie. She wasn't busy today. All the customers seemed to be getting pet pictures, fighting over parking spaces, and walking down the sidewalk with white bags and a large black paw print on the front. A few people peeked in the window at the model train making its way around the tracks in the front window, but most hurried by and back to their cars to avoid getting wet.

"This wouldn't have anything to do with a certain boy, would it?" Rylee stepped into the antique shop with Bryan. Bryan carried a large white bag with a paw print on it. A stuffed reindeer stuck out the top.

Bryan caught Ivy looking at the bag. "Dogs need presents too. We couldn't resist." He shrugged.

Ivy glanced down at Max who lay in his bed, chewing a hole in the side. White stuffing lay on the floor beside the bed. She obviously needed a few chew toys for Max.

"Have you taken Max for his Santa pictures?" Rylee stepped up to the counter. She wore a flannel jacket, a matching red hat, and jeans with work boots.

"We're not going," Ivy said, and clipped her lips together. She'd no need for a picture with Santa. She donated every year to the animal shelter and didn't need to get a silly pet photo, especially a Christmas photo.

"But it's so much fun," Rylee said. "We are going to use it for our holiday cards this year."

"Mine are already sent," Ivy said, her cards checked off her list last week. She sent the same card every year, varying only a color or an image. With the click of a button, the cards were delivered to all her vendors and distributors. She didn't have an extensive friend's list.

The holiday cards she received she hung around the small office doorway of her shop. Most of them included pictures of poinsettias or wreaths and generic holiday greetings inside. She'd seen the holiday card displays her friends had. Sasha placed hers around her home on small tabletop displays. Pictures of families on summer vacations, posed with children in front of waterfalls and beaches, pets posed alongside the family. Every year, Sasha took a picture of Tyler on their summer road trip down the coast or to Portland or Seattle. They posed together in silly hats and plastic eyeglasses in front of everything from museums to bridges. The best one was a picture in front of the Fremont Troll under the bridge in Seattle. But Ivy wasn't going to get all sentimental for the holidays. Christmas was business. A business that hers was not doing well with this year.

A loud bark came through the shared wall.

"Can I go?" Maddie asked. "Lars is counting on me." Maddie's cheeks flushed pink. Her eyes were bright.

"Yes," Ivy said. "Go on." She understood high school crushes. A high school crush that she never wanted to pursue more because that would have broken the friendship she treasured so much. But which she could never push the feelings deep enough to forget. After high school, as Josh and Kami became serious, she threw all her energy into rebuilding the run-down thrift store into a charming place to find a unique gift or item for the home.

She tried to hide her feelings for Josh deep into a place she didn't visit and worked hard to make The Red Door Antiques a successful business. It worked and each year her sales increased, until this year. But, she straightened her shoulders, there was still time before Christmas. Paws for a Cause was one weekend. Next weekend, the last weekend before Christmas, would be better. People tended to overspend in the days before Christmas as they hurried to find that perfect gift. It would all work out, she told herself.

"Be sure to bring Max for his photo!" Maddie dashed out the door as Josh walked in. "Cranberry Bay is having its day!" he said. A red Santa hat perched on his head. He wore a different holiday sweater, this one was green with a big elf in the middle with a stack of presents surrounding it.

Max shook himself off and walked out from behind the counter to greet Josh. Josh reached into his pocket and pulled out a dog bone. "You knew I had one!"

"You should take Max next door and get that picture," Rylee said. "Bryan and I will watch the shop."

"Thanks, but…"

"Great idea!" Josh said. "I'll go with you! Let's go get that holiday Paws for a Cause photo."

"Go on," Bryan said and took his place on the shop stool. He moved Max's bed out of the way with his foot. "Looks like Max needs a new bed."

Outnumbered by her friends and unable to protest when the shop was, in fact, very empty and there was nothing stopping her from going next door to take a pet photo with Santa, Ivy clipped Max's leash onto his collar. She didn't reach for her coat. She'd only be outside a brief minute. There was a door between Paige's shop and hers in the back. When Katie owned her fabric shop, they often left the door open and moved back and forth for quick breaks. But after Katie closed her sewing shop, Ivy hadn't wanted to open it. She kept the door locked on her side and never mentioned it to Paige.

Josh held open the front door. Outside, Ivy stopped while Max did his business on the grassy area outside the antique shop. The last thing she wanted was Max leaving behind a trail in the dog store. Max finished and sniffed the ground. Rain dropped on her shoulders, and she shivered.

"That's enough, Max," Josh said in a deep booming voice.

Max jumped to attention and pulled on the leash toward Josh.

Ivy smiled at Josh and ducked under Josh's arm as she scurried into the dog store. "Thanks. He seems to listen to you better than me."

Josh chuckled. "I have the treats."

Maddie sat at a large table and checked people in on a clipboard. A tall, thin boy who looked to be about sixteen, stood with a camera in front of Santa who sat in a plush red chair beside a large tree decorated in dog bones and dog ornaments. He snapped a white Bichon's picture who wore a small plaid collar around its neck. The owner, a tall, thin, petite woman with white hair that matched her dog, stood behind the teenagers taking the photo and held up a squeaky toy. She squeaked the toy and the dog looked at her. The photographer snapped the picture.

"Here." Josh slid a pair of reindeer ears on Max's head. "Now, he's ready for his picture."

Ivy tried to smile. It was just a picture. A picture that was going to a good cause. But her stomach churned. She didn't enjoy festive holiday events. They felt too out of control, too many opportunities for her to slip backward into painful childhood memories she didn't want to think about. The only holiday event she attended was the Holiday Express. She didn't even attend the annual Cranberry Bay tree lighting. Instead, preferring to stay in her shop's small office with a cup of tea and work on updating orders for her online shop.

"You made it!" Maddie wrote down Max's name on the clipboard. "You are in luck. There is only one person in front of you." She pointed toward a petite lady with a cat carrier.

"Uh oh." Ivy pulled Max away from the carrier. A tabby stared at him from inside and hissed. "I don't think this is such a good idea. Max has never met a cat."

"You can go to the training room," Maddie said. "There are some chairs set up and we'll call you."

Ivy marveled at Maddie's professionalism. She sounded like she'd been directing Santa photos for years.

Ivy pulled Max away from the table and the hissing cat. Max pulled her to a row of boxes filled with treats. Every box was open and ready to be eaten by whatever dog walked by. Max stuck his nose into one and chomped down on a treat. Ivy dragged Max away from the treats and pulled him toward the back of the store where Katie always kept her sewing machines for classes.

The room was empty except for a set of chairs sat in a circle. Ivy sat down in one of the folding chairs and tried to pull Max toward her. He jerked the other way. She tugged hard on the leash and his collar tightened. His paws skid on the concrete floor.

Josh sat down beside her and pulled another treat out of his pocket.

"The real Santa," Ivy said as Max gobbled the treat.

Josh leaned closer and Ivy inhaled the scent of a spicy aftershave or shampoo. She drifted along on the warmth radiating from Josh's body.

"Ivy?" Maddie poked her head into the training room. "We're ready for you. The cat didn't want to get out of the carrier."

Ivy stood, shook herself like Max, and followed Maddie into the store and Santa.

When she reached Santa, Max skidded backward and away from Santa's outstretched hand.

Josh leaned down and pushed Max forward.

Max pushed hard against Josh and whined.

"I don't think this is going to work." Ivy knew Santa photos were a bad idea for Max. He was too skittish, too much a puppy with no training.

"It's okay." Paige stepped forward with a treat. She placed her hand on Max's back and stroked him. "A lot of dogs are scared of Santa." Paige wore a green and red full apron over jeans and a red sweater. The apron didn't look like one of Katie's or the sewing circle aprons. A small tag hung on the pocket with a small store brand label. She probably bought it at some specialty shop in Seattle who sold forty-dollar aprons and claimed they were handmade.

Max stopped pulling away and pulled toward Paige and her treat.

"Just like the Pied Piper!" Josh said.

Paige smiled at him and said, "Something like that. We're ready for the photo, Lars," Paige directed the lanky teenage boy with the camera.

Lars took Max's leash and led the dog to Santa. Max wagged his tail as Santa offered him more treats. Max stayed focus on Lars and didn't need the squeaky toy trick to focus him to the camera.

Lars snapped a couple pictures as Paige turned to Ivy. "Why don't you hop into the next picture? Pets love to have their owners with them."

Ivy stepped forward and stood beside Santa. Max pulled toward Josh.

"No, Max," Ivy reached into her pocket but came up empty-handed. She hadn't remembered to refill her pockets with treats.

"I've got it," Josh stepped forward, slipped his hand into his pocket and held out a treat to Max.

Max wagged his tail and chewed.

"Why don't you join them in the picture?" Paige said. "I don't think Max is going to let you step away without following you." Her laughter filled the room.

Ivy stiffened as Josh stepped behind her and placed

his hand on her lower back. It was just a friendly gesture. Nothing more between two friends. His strong presence stood behind her, steadying her.

Santa looked very familiar and winked at Ivy.

Ivy smiled at Tom. He'd found a way to play Santa this year, even if it wasn't on the train.

"Come on, good boys and girls." He held out his arm. "Let's all get a picture together with Max!"

Ivy kneeled on one side of Santa and Josh stood behind her. Max leaned against Santa's side. Josh placed his hand on the top of Ivy's shoulder.

"Perfect!" Paige said.

Lars snapped pictures. "I've really got some good ones!"

Josh squeezed her shoulder. "Doing great."

Ivy wasn't sure if he was talking to her or Max.

After a few more photos, Max pulled away from Santa and shook himself off.

"I think we're done." Ivy stood up and took a step backward into Josh. His arm came around her waist to steady her. She froze, breathing in his deep, musky scent as his body pressed against hers.

Max dragged his leash across the floor as he made his way to Lars and Maddie who knelt and each gave him another treat.

Ivy stepped away from Josh. Her heart pounded with the feelings racing inside. This was exactly why it was not good to engage in holiday events. It shattered her held-together emotions and brought up feelings of longing, feelings with no chance of ever working out with Josh.

"Your picture is ready." Lars lifted a picture from the printer and handed it to Ivy. "We can also email you a copy so you can share it digitally."

Ivy took the picture Lars held out.

In the picture, Josh stood behind her, a smile on his lips, his hand pressed on her shoulder.

"That's a wonderful picture," Paige said. "The two of you are just a natural couple together."

Ivy flushed. She reached in her pocket to pull out a twenty-dollar bill and dropped it in the glass jar on the counter with Donations printed on the side.

"It's a wonderful thing you're doing," Ivy said, her voice sounding stiff and unnatural. "I'm sure the animal shelter will appreciate the donations."

"Yes!" Paige clapped her hands together. "It's been a wonderful, successful weekend. We're planning to do it again next weekend."

"Next weekend?" Ivy froze. If Paige did the Paws for a Cause next weekend too, her shop would suffer another weekend of slow sales on the last weekend before Christmas.

"I've already told Anne at the Chamber," Paige said. "Everyone is very excited, and they've scheduled marketing posts on their social media."

"I see." Ivy picked up Max's leash as images of her plummeting sales flashed in front of her. "Next weekend is the Holiday Homes Tour." She didn't add it was her signature event, the event which brought people into her shop and looking for items to decorate their homes in the same manner and style as the ones on the tour. Her card was attached to every home on the tour, displayed on front tables and large dining room tables in antique glass bowls. She always received emails and calls about specific items people wanted her to find for their home, items they'd seen on the tour.

"That's even better," Paige said, her voice raised in excitement. "We will have more people in town who will want pictures. Every dollar counts to help the animals!"

"Mmmm…." Ivy didn't mention that every dollar donated helped the animals. The dollars spent on gifts for pets went to Paige's business. Pet owners who brought their dogs and cats for Paws for A Claus weren't going to wander in her store. All dogs must be leashed to wander the crowded aisles with overstuffed vendor booths. The vendors didn't carry items that catered to pet owners. There were no vintage leashes, collars, or dog toys.

She turned away from Paige. Colorful flyers hung from a bulletin board by the front counter. Upcoming dog obedience classes, nose work, some basic agility, and training for reading therapy teams. Ivy stepped closer and peered at the flyer.

"Lots of good trainings coming up," Paige said. "Max is just at the perfect age to be involved in our classes. It's good socializing for the dogs."

"You're training for the reading therapy dog team!" Josh leaned over Ivy's shoulder. "We use the teams at the elementary school. The kids love when the dog comes to school. It's so calming and reassuring to have a dog to read to."

Ivy bit her lip. Could a reading therapy dog help her

with her anxieties about reading for the Holiday Express? Maybe she could check out a stack of library books and practice reading to Max.

Josh picked up a squeaky Santa and held it in the air with a loud squeak. Max wagged his tail and barked. Josh placed it on the counter. "I'll take this," he said. "And a large bag of those treats you were giving out."

"You don't have to do that," Ivy stepped forward. "I can pay for it."

"Yes," Josh placed his hand on Ivy's. "It's Christmas. This is Max's present." He squeezed her hand. "I want to do this."

"That's so nice!" Maddie handed her the photo of her and Josh in a red envelope. "I wrote your store email down and we'll send you a digital copy too. You can share it on the store's social media! The customers will love it."

Josh leaned over her shoulder and peered at the picture. "A perfect holiday photo!"

Ivy's stomach danced. She couldn't share this photo. Everyone would assume she and Josh were a couple. And they were not. They were friends and friends did not look like this photo. They did not gaze at each other with a longing which spoke of so much more emotion than friendship. The best thing to do with this photo was to lose it under a stack of to-do lists and delete the email with the digital photo.

Chapter 8

A few evenings later, Maddie clicked the switch beside the Red Door Antique shop's front door and the outdoor twinkle lights turned on. The wreath's lights turned on with the setting sun and the darkening late afternoon sky. "I can't wait for the tree lighting tonight."

"Mmm." Ivy wrapped a box of antique ornaments in tissue paper and placed them inside a white bag with the Red Door Antiques gold sticker on the outside of the bag. She threaded the bag with a red ribbon and handed it to the tall, dark-haired woman standing on the other side of the counter. The tree lighting was never something she enjoyed, and often found work she needed to do instead of attending.

Maddie leaned over and picked a glass turquoise ornament off the floor. She hung it beside a pink one on the artificial white tree.

"The tree lighting is one of the best parts of Cranberry Bay holidays," the woman said. "My sisters and I come to Cranberry Bay every year from Seaview Cove. We love staying at the River Rock Inn."

"The rooms in the Inn are always so beautifully decorated." Another woman stepped up to the counter and looped her arms through her sister's. "But we just like to be together at the holidays."

A small ache formed in the pit of Ivy's chest. Christmas had never been her favorite time of the year. But her brother worked hard to make sure they were always together. The few times she attended the tree lighting was because Keith and Josh convinced her to go. This year, without him, she wasn't planning to attend the tree lighting.

A crash of shattering glass filled the air.

Ivy turned to find the box of ornaments that a customer left on a small side table, lying shattered on the ground.

"I'm sorry," Maddie's face reddened. "I'll pay for everything. You can take it out of my paycheck."

Ivy ducked into her office and grabbed the broom and dustpan. When she returned, the sisters were gone. "There are a few here that didn't break." Ivy gingerly picked them up and placed them on the counter. "Not all is lost."

Tears bubbled in Maddie's eyes, and she looked away from Ivy.

Ivy peered closer at her. "Are you okay?"

Maddie nodded, leaned down and scooped a large piece of broken ornament into her palm. When she placed it on the counter, a small drop of blood fell from her left finger.

"You're hurt." Ivy reached under the counter and pulled out the First Aid kit she kept under the counter. Opening a small package of antiseptic, she wiped Maddie's finger and then placed a band-aid on her finger.

Maddie glanced out the window at the crowd gathering around a large fir tree overlooking the river. "Can I go to the tree lighting now? I want to get a good spot."

"Of course." Most people didn't want to stand on the edge of the cliff, where half the tree stood, and wanted to get a good picture of the tree lighting from the front side. But the space in front of the tree wasn't that big, and with all the rain in the last couple weeks, the saturated ground made the space even smaller.

"Are you coming?" Maddie pulled on her coat and a pair of fluffy red and green mittens.

"I have some things I need to do here." Despite the begging and pleading by her friends, the tree lighting was not something she enjoyed. The happy families, the couples, all gathered around the tree, waiting to see the moment when the lights lit it up. All of it filling her heart with an ache of what she missed at Christmas.

"Can you flip the sign to closed?" Ivy asked as Maddie headed toward the door. "And turn the lock?"

After the lock clicked behind Maddie, Ivy walked to her office where there was a small heating plate. She turned it on under a small kettle. Earlier in the day, she'd filled the kettle with water and now it only took a few minutes for it to warm. Picking up a small basket of teas, she shifted through them until she found peppermint. As she waited for the hot water to heat, Ivy pulled up her computer and logged into her Etsy account. There were only a handful of new orders waiting to be filled. The last two days were busy with orders coming in, but not frantic. Her online store was operating better than in her in-shop purchases, but it wasn't enough to bring the shop into the black for the year. It was time to offer some substantial discounts and free shipping. She clicked through her page and marked a handful of items to qualify for free shipping. She marked another dozen items for discounts. The sound of carolers drifted from outside the shop as the annual caroling party made their way down Main Street. Ivy knew Gracie would be leading the carolers. It was her favorite holiday thing to do, one she started a few years ago. The singers gathered in the River Rock Inn front room around the piano and warmed up before heading out to the tree lighting.

Ivy shut her office door and poured hot water over her tea bag. For the first time in weeks, it was quiet next door. There weren't any dogs barking in training classes, and crowds of people weren't waiting in line to buy a holiday toy for their pet. Max shifted on his new dog bed, and she handed him a few treats to keep him in his bed. It worked and he sat with his paws in front of him, looking expectedly at her for more. She read over her to-do list, printed and posted on a clipboard beside her. She had plenty to check off tonight and by the time she finished with her list, the tree lighting would be over for another year. A small ache filled her as for a minute she imagined what it would be like to go to the tree lighting, sip hot cocoa from Sasha's food cart, laugh with Katie and Rylee, and look into the sparkling eyes of Josh as he gazed down at her. She shook her head. She wasn't going to allow herself to engage in silly romantic holiday dreams. It was best to keep her mind focused on her to do lists.

JOSH STOOD at the far-left side of the large, twenty-foot spruce that towered over the river's bluff. The lights along the walkway twinkled. A crowd gathered, most of them settling on the right side of the tree which provided the best viewpoint for the lighting. Bundled in their winter coats, hats, and scarves it was hard to tell who was who, but occasionally a familiar voice drifted over to him. He knew not to look for Ivy— she didn't enjoy attending the tree lighting. Before he took his police officer job, Keith often helped with crowd control and directed parking beside what used to be a set of run-down fishing cottages before Rylee and Bryan renovated them. He once asked Keith why she didn't want to attend, but Keith became closed-lipped and changed the subject. Josh didn't press for information. There were some things better kept between siblings, no matter how close the friendship.

Now, children's voices called through the night as they stood in line in front of a red and white vintage trailer where Sasha served hot cocoa and cookies. Tyler leaned halfway out of the window with a plate of cookies. A green elf hat dangled off his head. Sasha reached out and yanked him back inside the food cart. She placed the tray of cookies on the front window ledge. Josh smiled. He loved children's energy and excitement at Christmas.

Katie and Sawyer stood near the food cart as Sawyer's ten-year-old daughter, Lauren, bounced up and down on one foot and then the other. She wore a matching elf hat to Tyler. Both would be elves on the Holiday Express for the first time this season, and by the looks of things, neither could wait.

Josh refocused on the electrical box in front of him. For days, he worked with Adam to check each strand and link them together down the twenty-foot tree. They used a rented articulating boom lift with an ariel platform and a bendable joined arm attached to a turn table. Each one taking turns on the platform to attach the lights and check the connections.

"How's it coming?" Mayor Mays asked. His wife, Amy, stood nearby with their twins, bundled in blankets in a stroller.

"We're just about there." Josh flicked the light switches. The switches operated on similar electrical wiring to his grandfather's train sets. A few years ago, his grandpa rewired the lights to the tree box, making a few changes in the controls to ensure that if one strand didn't turn on, another switch could take over its place.

A dog nosed Josh's leg and he looked down to Raisin who wore a red blinking collar. Bryan pulled him away from Josh's leg. "Need any help?"

Josh shook his head. "I think we're good."

The carolers circled around the tree, singing, *Oh Christmas Tree.*

When they finished, Mayor Mays spoke with the microphone. "Good evening, Cranberry Bay! Merry Christmas!"

Voices of all ages called back, "Merry Christmas!"

"I'd like to start by thanking the Cranberry Bay Business Association for fundraising for a new star this year. As you know, our old one was blown off the tree and into the river last year and we were in desperate need of a new tree topper."

Cheers and claps filled the air.

"I'd also like to take a few minutes and acknowledge a couple men who make this tree lighting possible every year. Rain or shine, they hang the lights so we can have this beautiful ceremony. Adam Shuster and Josh Morton."

The small ground spotlight beamed at Josh. He raised his hand and waved. Then the spotlight moved toward Adam, standing on the other side of the tree.

"Now," Mayor Mays said. "The moment you've all been waiting for."

Josh's heart pounded. He squatted at the switch box.

"One, two, three," he counted under his breath.

Josh pulled the lever.

The lights filled the tree in a colorful display of red, green, and white. Applause and cheers filled the air.

Josh took a deep breath.

"And now the star," Mayor Mays said.

Josh stepped over the tree light cords attached to a running generator and hit the small button. He looked upward. The star didn't light.

The crowd became still and silent.

"Let's try that again," Mayor Mays said. "How about we give Josh a little more light?"

The spotlight circled around him to show the set of cords attached to the generator.

Josh pushed the button whose small wires were attached to the star on top of the tree. The star remained dark.

"Why don't we have some more carols?" Mayor Mays said. "We'll give Josh and Adam a few minutes to see what's happening."

The choral group broke into *We Wish You a Merry Christmas* and the crowd followed suit. The line by Sasha's food truck grew longer.

Sawyer and Bryan arrived at the side of the tree at the same time.

"Is there a short in the star?" Sawyer pulled out his cell phone. "I'll make a few calls. See if we can get an electrician over here as soon as possible." As one of the area's premier builders, Sawyer kept all the plumbers and electrician's numbers at his fingertips. Most of them would usually do whatever job he asked, especially with Sawyer's tacked on cash bonus.

"We tested the star before we put it on the tree," Adam said. "Everything worked fine."

Josh jiggled a few more levers on the tree. The lights flickered but the star didn't light.

The crowd murmured and a few people drifted back toward their cars.

"Everything going to be okay tonight?" Mayor Mays asked from the makeshift stand in front of the tree.

"We're going to have to get on the boom lifter tomorrow," Adam said. "We can't fix this in the dark."

Mayor Mays turned on the mic. "Sorry, folks. We've got a little malfunction with the star. We'll get it lit by tomorrow."

A collective groan of disappointment filled the crowd.

"Sorry, sorry." Mayor Mays set the mic down and motioned toward the carolers to sing. "But the tree will be lit for the next couple of weeks. Bring your family and friends and enjoy!"

Sounds of *Joy to the World* filled the night sky, but the music fell flat on Josh's ears. He looked toward the darkened Main Street and the Red Door Antique shop. He was glad Ivy wasn't at the tree lighting to see his failure.

———

THE NEXT MORNING, Josh rode his bike through the early morning darkened streets of Cranberry Bay. He wore his orange reflective jacket over his jeans, pull-over sweater, and fleece jacket. A slight pinkening to the sky emerged beyond the mountains, but it would take another couple hours before morning dawned in Cranberry Bay. The lighted tree, minus the star, stood tall against the black sky. The timer was set to turn the lights off at sunrise.

Josh peddled hard up the steep hill toward the elementary school, inhaling the cold air into his lungs. It'd been a long evening of working with Adam to figure out why the star didn't light. Sawyer's electrician joined them, but no one could find the short in the star. Finally, frozen with cold, all of them trooped into the pub to nurse their disappointment with a couple beers. That afternoon, he'd meet with Adam and they'd get the star and bring it down. If the star was broken or defective, it was too late to order another one. The star came from the East Coast, and they had ordered in August. This year's tree would have to stand without a tree topper, a disappointment to Cranberry Bay and the beloved holiday traditions.

When Josh got to school, he pulled his bike around to the side where a couple of bike racks stood close to his classroom windows. The racks were mainly for students but at this time of the year, few students were riding their bikes to school. Josh inserted his lock and clicked his bike to the steel rack. He pulled open the large double doors and headed toward his class.

"Josh!" Anne stuck her head out the faculty room door. "Sorry about the tree lighting last night."

Josh's stomach plummeted. He knew his students would want to know what happened, but he hoped to spend most of his day away from the other staff, buried in his classroom.

"Gavin says you should return that star immediately and get a new one."

Josh shook his head. "Afraid we can't do that. The

star was ordered from New York. We checked to see if they had any more in stock but doesn't look like they'd get it to us in time for Christmas."

"Mr. Morton!" Mason hurled his backpack down the hall. It slid all the way to Josh's feet and stopped.

"Mason!" Anne said, her voice fierce with determination. "That is no way to walk down these halls. Go get your backpack. Pick it up and let's try that again."

"Sorry!" Mason ran down the hall and skidded across the shiny wood floors. "Are you in trouble because the star didn't light?"

"Mason," Anne strode up to the boy. "The star not lighting is not Mr. Morton's fault. And I don't want to hear one more word about it, okay?"

"But…" Mason said.

"No." Anne put her finger to her lips. "It's time for you to head to the library. You're a little early and the buses aren't here yet, so we aren't sending kids to the cafeteria for breakfast.

"But…"

Anne placed her hand on Jack's lower back and steered him in the direction of the library. She turned to Josh. "If you have any problems today with any of the students, in your class or not, please immediately send them my way."

"Josh!" Celia, the art teacher, pulled open the heavy double doors at the end of the hall. A guest of wind blew in with her. "What happened at the tree lighting? The star didn't light?

"Sorry," Anne said. "You're on your own with the

staff." She smiled at him and strode down the hall and toward the front doors of the building where the first buses were beginning to make their way into the circular driveway.

"Faulty star," Josh said, not smiling.

"Such a shame." Celia took off her knit hat and shook out her hair. "I hope the rest of Cranberry Bay's Christmas events go as planned." She lowered her voice. "My niece and nephew are coming to visit for the holidays. They are so excited about the Holiday Express. It'd be a shame if something happened to that too."

"I'm sure the Holiday Express will go on as planned." Josh turned toward his classroom and opened the door. He flicked on the lights and shut the door firmly behind him. He sank down at his desk and stared at his stack of ungraded math papers. He understood the disappointment and anxiety about the tree. The tree lighting had always gone off without a problem, until now.

His phone beeped inside his pocket, and he pulled it out.

I found a star. Ivy texted. *I put a rush order and the star should arrive in two days.*

Josh exhaled. Despite Ivy's resistance to attend the tree lighting, she used her keen ability to scour online retailers for exactly what was needed. The tree lighting may not have happened on the night it was supposed to, but it would still happen. The people of Cranberry Bay would get their tree, and with Ivy's help, he would also make sure they got the Holiday Express tradition too.

He texted her back a red heart as his own lifted.

Chapter 9

Ivy checked the delivery progress of the star tree topper. Nothing had changed since the last time she checked, two hours ago. The package just left Michigan and should arrive in Cranberry Bay in another forty-eight hours. She closed her laptop and slid it into her over-the-shoulder bag beside her large bag, filled with fleece fabric. She double checked her hot plate, making sure it was turned off, and slipped into her coat. Hefting both bags to her shoulders, Ivy made her way to the front door, straightening an item here and there. She turned on the picture window light and placed the train in the front of the window on the tracks, but with the lever turned off.

Outside, she inhaled the cold night air. A light mist fell. The spruce tree stood tall on the riverbank, its lights twinkling in the early dark evening. Although she never enjoyed the tree lighting with all its festivities, she did enjoy the tree once it was lit. The lights twinkled in a triangular shape up and down the tree, and the top was dark. She knew something was wrong during the tree lighting. The festive carols and voices fell silent. It only took one glance out the window to see the lit tree and the black space on the peak of the tree.

Ivy logged into a couple of her favorite online vendors. It hadn't taken long for a tree topper star to pop up in a small town in Michigan. The town hadn't been able to raise enough money to fund a tree lighting. The tradition ended and the large ornaments, lights and tree topper were placed in a warehouse. The warehouse was currently being emptied to make way for a new boat storage company. The star was practically given to her, and she only needed to pay for shipping. She declined the large glittery ornaments, knowing that they would easily blow away in the wind on the bluff. But a few extra strands of lights didn't hurt, and she'd paid for those along with the postage.

Ivy headed around the backside of the building and unlocked her car. She tossed her bags on the passenger seat. She eyed the upstairs window of the building. She settled Max, tucked into the couch pillows, in her small apartment above the antique store. He'd be settled for the next few hours as she worked with the sewing circle to finish the lazy pajama pants for the Holiday Express.

Ivy pulled out of the parking lot and drove down Main Street and away from the festive holiday lights. It didn't take long to reach the end of town and the rolling dark fields stretched before her. This past year, Sawyer and Adam worked with the state parks and railroad to expand the bike trail onto paved old railroads. The bike trails were popular, and families often spent the long summer days biking. But now, only darkness stretched before her, something she tried to avoid especially at this time of the year. She hit a button on her radio and holiday tunes filled her car. Ivy reached to change the station to one of her playlists, but before she could, *Jingle Bells Rock* filled the car. Ivy smiled and returned her hands to the steering wheel. She tapped the wheel in tune with the music. It was hard to forget that the song was Josh's favorite in high school. She could still see him dancing around the high school gymnasium as they worked on sorting the collected canned soups for the food pantry, *Soups for Santa*, one of Josh's projects on the student body government.

Ivy hummed as she pulled into Katie's long driveway. The barn glowed with strands of white lights hanging around the exterior. A couple lighted deer gazed alongside the pathway. The large two-story home was lit in red and green lights hanging from the second floor and a huge blow-up Santa danced in the light breeze beside the sweeping front porch. Two wreaths with red bows hung on the front doors. Even Katie's vintage RV had a strand of lights running around the exterior. Behind the barn, Lisa's small cottage home also sported a strand of lights on its deck and the antique sleigh Maddie confiscated from the antique shop's back room looked perfect on the front porch with a small plastic Santa plugged into an outlet by the front door.

The whole scene looked like something out of a

Norman Rockwell Holiday. Ivy smiled. She was happy for Katie. Although she missed Katie's shop next door, especially at this time of the year, Katie's business took off with the extra space in the barn and the support from Sawyer. Katie glowed with the love of a family surrounding her.

Ivy parked the car alongside Sasha's Toyota truck. She gathered her bags and walked to the barn. As she pulled open the double doors, holiday music greeted her, the smell of cinnamon from a candle, and the voices of her friends as they worked on the Holiday Express lazy pants.

"Ivy!" Gracie jumped up from her spot at the table where she was cutting fabric. She walked over and embraced her. "We were just beginning to worry."

"Sorry." Ivy dropped her fabric bag on the table and tucked her computer bag underneath one of the table legs. "I had to wrap up some last-minute things at the shop."

"We heard you found a star!" Katie's eyes glowed.

"It will be here the day after tomorrow." Ivy sat down at the table. "I had no idea that when a town discontinues its annual tree lighting, everything just gets tossed in a warehouse and forgotten."

"I hope we never have to find that out in Cranberry Bay," Rylee said, taking a bite of one of Sasha's gingerbread cookies.

"You really saved the day," Katie said. "You know how Cranberry Bay is about its holiday traditions!"

"And you don't even like the tree lighting!" Sasha

murmured as she walked past Ivy, clutching a pair of red lazy pants to her chest.

Ivy busied herself and pushed the left leg of the flannel pant through her sewing machine while keeping one eye on her cell phone. In all the flurry of locating the tree topper and placing the order, she'd forgotten about the holiday party invites she'd sent out to her vendors. But now, she waited anxiously for responses. She sent out ten invitations and not one responded.

"That seam is a little crocked, Ivy." Katie set a stack of fleece pants on top of her phone.

Ivy pushed the stack out of the way. She willed her phone to show one message, just one.

"Are you waiting for someone special to message you?" Katie winked.

"None of the vendors have responded to the holiday party," Ivy said. "I sent the invitation a week ago and not one response."

"It's a busy time of the year," Gracie said. "Not everyone checks their emails."

"They weren't emails," Ivy said. "I made each invitation. We received a large basket of holiday thank you cards and party invites. I used ten of them for the vendor holiday party."

"The post office is slow this time of year," Katie said. "I'm waiting on a couple invoices from my suppliers who refuse to invoice me through email."

"Right," Ivy bit her lower lip. "Not even Jill Malone has responded, and she always responds to everything immediately."

"Don't worry," Katie dropped her arm around Ivy's shoulders. She squeezed. "I'm sure you'll have a great turnout for the holiday party. It's a great thing to do for all your vendors."

"Mmm." Ivy nodded while a little pit of black darkness formed in her stomach. It would be a busy week with the Historic Homes Tour, the vendor holiday tea, and then the Holiday Express, but that was what she wanted. She wanted to get to Christmas Day and curl up on the couch with a mug of hot cocoa and watch all the movies she could fit in during a one-day period. She didn't want to have to remember it was Christmas and she was alone.

Her phone beeped and she grabbed it. *Thanks for the invite. It looks like a fun party, but the kids are back from college, and I want to spend as much time as possible with them.* Jill Marson texted.

"Well," Ivy dropped her phone face side down. "I guess the invites have reached people. Just got my first no."

"Don't worry," Gracie said. "I'm sure people will start responding yes. It's a busy time and you're bound to get a couple who can't make it."

A gust of cold wind blew in as Rylee pulled open the barn doors and stepped inside. A tall, broad-shouldered woman with dark hair walked in after her.

"Look who I found at the tree lighting last night!" Rylee exclaimed.

Raisin bounded into the room, running straight for the small kitchen area where he immediately put his paws on the counter and used his snout to reach for a spritz cookie from a plate.

"Raisin!" Rylee rushed into the kitchen and removed her dog from the counter. She attached his leash and led him over to one of the two plush dog beds in the corner of the room. Katie always kept a couple of dog beds in the barn. She said it was for the dogs of her friends, but Ivy suspected Katie was trying to hint to Sawyer she wanted a dog.

"Suzanne!" Katie rushed over and embraced her.

"Well, that's the end of our fun," Sasha muttered under her breath.

Ivy turned to her. "Shhh. She'll hear you."

"I don't care," Sasha shrugged. "Everyone knows how I feel about her."

Suzanne and Sasha's rivalry dated back to high school when Suzanne won a school-wide cookie competition. No one expected the school's swim star win a cookie contest, but when she walked in a pan of chocolate covered nut bars, the votes poured into the ballot box.

Sasha insisted the ballot box was stuffed, the school needed a recount, and nothing could be better than her chocolate chip double fudge brownies.

But the votes were clear. Suzanne won. And Sasha's dislike for Suzanne was sealed.

Suzanne shrugged out of a long cream trench coat and Katie took it from her and hung it on a row of coat hooks near the front door.

"I don't really sew," Suzanne said. "Mom wanted to teach me, but I was always too busy to learn."

"Right," Sasha said, not so quietly. "Like you don't really cook."

Suzanne ignored her and walked over to Ivy. She peered over her shoulder. "You have always been such a great seamstress. I remember how you sewed all your clothes."

Ivy plastered on a smile. She hadn't sewn all her clothes because she wanted to, she'd sewn them because that was how she knew how to survive. It was very obvious, by the time she was in middle school, that clothing money wasn't something her foster families could afford. She and Keith received donated clothes that didn't fit or were cheaply made and fell apart. Her middle school art teacher encouraged her to start sewing. Ms. Madoff kept a small sewing machine set up on a back corner table, and Ivy enjoyed arriving early to school and trying simple things like pillowcases and bags.

In high school, Ivy found an old Singer sewing machine at the Goodwill. Her brother fixed a few parts and she began sewing her clothes. When she found the embroidery machine in a secondhand shop, she sewed embroidered flowers onto jeans and jackets. Her clothing became a hit at school, and she took orders and tucked the money away in a small envelope in her dresser drawer. After high school, she used the money to take a couple business classes at the local community center which helped her keep the books at the antique shop.

Ivy couldn't wait to give the sewing circle their gifts this year. She'd been working on art quilts for each one of them. Using fabric paints she created colorful squares of muslin with flower designs and sewed each square together. Each quilt was specially designed with the colors each woman used in their home.

"Suzanne, why don't you help us with the cutting?" Katie asked. "We still have a good number of tops to cut out."

"How is coaching?" Gracie asked from her spot in the comfortable chair by the stone fireplace. A log crackled inside. She made the final tucks on each pair of lazy pants and sewed in the special fabric Holiday Express label.

A shadow passed over Susanne's face before she answered, her voice controlled. "I've got a great group of swimmers this season."

"How long are you in town?" Sasha asked.

"For the holidays," Suzanne said, the same bright, controlled tone filling her voice. She didn't meet anyone's eyes and picked up a flimsy pattern and lay it over the fleece.

"Here," Katie stepped beside her. "If you lay it across the fabric like this, we can get another one cut out of this fabric too."

"Right," Suzanne nodded, her face flushed.

Ivy felt sad for Suzanne. Even though swimming was her passion, it still couldn't be easy to be so focused on one thing.

The room filled with the sounds of sewing machines and scissors snipping.

After a few minutes, Suzanne raised her head and

looked at Ivy. "I hear you are going to be Mrs. Claus this year on the Holiday Express."

"Yes," Ivy nodded. She didn't have a grudge against Suzanne like Sasha. Suzanne was always nice to her when she was home.

"You're going to be Mrs. Claus?" Sasha dropped her coffee with a hard thump on the wood table. "Why didn't you tell us?"

"It just happened," Ivy's face flushed. "At the board meeting the other night."

"You do not have time to sew these lazy pants and tops," Sasha walked over and jerked Ivy's half-finished pant leg from under the sewing machine. The thread spooled out in a long trail beside the fabric. "You need a costume to play Mrs. Claus!"

"I was just going to alter the one Maureen always wore," Ivy said. She did not need a new Mrs. Claus dress. She was only playing Mrs. Claus for one year while Maureen and Tom were in Seattle. She could wear the red pinafore over the gingham dress, shorten it, take out some of the fabric around the sides, and when she was done, she'd make sure it was back to the measurements Maureen needed.

"Where is the red fabric? Sasha pulled open the large double doors leading to a closet where Katie stored fabric. "Or how about some gingham fabric?" Sasha eyed Ivy. "You would look great in a little gingham skirt with overall straps and a white blouse that has a scoop neckline."

Katie walked into the closet behind Sasha and pulled

out a bolt of red gingham fabric, a bolt of red velvet fabric, and a bolt of louse lacey white fabric. "These will be perfect. "

"I will pay you for all of this fabric," Ivy reached down to grab her computer bag where she tucked her slim wallet.

"No, you will not." Katie nodded her head. "This is on me. "

"I can't take all this fabric," Ivy eyed the white lacey blouse and red velvet fabric.

"Yes," Katie said. "You are filling a very important role for Cranberry Bay with the Holiday Express. There is no Holiday Express Train without Santa and his Mrs. Claus."

"I wanted to be Mrs. Claus," Suzanne said, a wistful longing in her voice.

"It's fun to play one of the roles for the Holiday Express," Katie said, her voice clipped and firm. "But you know this town, they don't like change."

"She's right," Gracie said, snipping a long thread of embroidery floss. "Ivy has been part of the Holiday Express since high school. It will be a natural fit for her to play Mrs. Claus in place of Maureen."

"My swimming has taken so much," Suzanne said. Her voice dropped an octave and sadness crept into the room. "I never thought it would be like this. I wouldn't have—" her voice trailed off and she didn't finish.

Ivy peered at Suzanne. Her face darkened with a deep shadow, and dark circles lined her eyes. Something was wrong with Suzanne. She made a mental note to talk to Josh. Josh and Suzanne weren't as close as she and Keith were as siblings. Maybe he didn't realize that Suzanne was struggling.

"I'm sorry. I just have a lot on my mind. I know how much this town misses my grandpa. I miss him too." Suzanne swallowed hard.

"We know you do." Katie walked over to Suzanne and gave her a hug. "There are other roles. I could use a hand with supervising the children as they are getting off the train and moving into Santa's workshop for story hour."

Story hour. Ivy's stomach lurched as if she was on a fast-moving train about to crash into the bluff. Maybe if she spent a couple days practicing the stories she'd be reading, she would feel confident. She did not want to let the children of Cranberry Bay down, and she fingered the soft fabric between her thumb and index finger, she didn't want to let Josh down.

Chapter 10

Josh turned the Great Northern orange model train box car over and ran his fingers alongside the wheels. "This is almost in perfect condition. Where did you find it?"

"I'm not sure which box." Ivy waved her hand toward the multiple boxes beside the counter. "Maddie and I still have quite a few to go through. One of the Seashore Cove families cleaned out their grandparent's home in Portland. They were avid collectors."

Josh picked up a miniature plastic fir tree. He peered out the front window of the Red Door Antique shop. The new star tree topper sparkled in the darkening early evening sky. If it hadn't been for Ivy, the tree would have remained without a tree topper. His heart filled with gratitude.

"I'm heading over to the tree farm to pick out a tree tonight. Want to join me?" The small tree farm on the outskirts of Cranberry Bay had finally grown enough trees to open for the season. The last couple years of too dry and hot summers hadn't produced a strong crop of Christmas trees.

Ivy wiped her hand across her forehead. "There's a lot to unpack here. I want to get some of this to the vendors. They've really been fighting me this season about not helping them out. Every single one of them said no to the holiday tea."

"No one is coming to the holiday tea?" Josh peered at Ivy. Ivy's holiday tea party for her vendors was a tradition at the Red Door Antique. It started the year she received a large donation of antique teacups from Mrs. Bonn's daughter. Unable to sell most of them, Ivy made a couple pots of peppermint tea, ordered boxes of cookies from Sasha's bakery, and invited the vendors to enjoy a holiday treat. The vendors loved using the old teacups and began setting aside teacups for the holiday party each year.

"No," Ivy's voice hardened. "They are upset with me because I have been telling them their prices are too high and nothing is selling."

"And she gave away donated things on the social media Buy Nothing group." Maddie opened a box and held up a pair of knitting needles and a skein of yarn. "I've always wanted to learn to knit!"

"Keep them," Ivy said. "Part of the benefits of unpacking the donations!"

"You gave away things in a Buy Nothing group?" Josh raised his eyebrow and grinned. He loved the Buy Nothing groups. He used them all the time for his classroom. He'd been able to score bean bags, packs of lined notebook paper, and even a carton of tissues.

"Not everything belongs in the store," Ivy said. "And it's good business to give away things. But I can't give away what belongs to the vendors. I only give away the general donated items that come into the store."

"Gotta side with you on this one," Josh walked to the window and placed the miniature tree beside the model train platform in the window. "How about picking out that tree with me? Can I pull you away from the store for a little bit?"

"I can stay late and unpack the boxes!" Maddie held a box of red and green ornaments in her hand. "I'll just call Mom and let her know. She has her last online business class of the term tonight and will be glad to have me out of her way."

"But Max…" Ivy said. "I think the tree lot is too much for him."

"I'll watch him." Maddie leaned down and ran her hand over the dog's back. He wagged his tail and gazed up at Maddie.

"It's settled," Josh said, and winked at Maddie.

Ivy exhaled. "I'll get my coat. I can see I'm outnumbered."

Ivy turned and walked into the office. Small white lights sparkled around the office doorway.

"Thanks for your help," Josh said to Maddie. He peered into the glass cabinet filled with antique Christmas pins. Silver, gold, and green tree pins filled the case with a few snowmen, a couple Santas, and a handful of candy cane shaped pins. His grandmother always wore a green tree pin with small glass red beads that looked like sparkling ornaments. After she died, the pin passed to his mom, but he couldn't remember the last time he saw her wear it.

"I'm ready." Ivy stepped out of the office. She wore a soft red knit hat and a green down jacket with a hood.

"How much is that pin?" Josh pointed to a small white snowman. He didn't have a gift for Suzanne and the snowman reminded him of the year it snowed in Cranberry Bay when they were children. Unlike other snows that melted in a day, temperatures remained low and it snowed for a week. He and Suzanne, along with a couple other neighborhood kids, built snowmen in every yard that would let them. It was one of the few Christmases he could remember that he felt close to Suzanne.

Ivy twisted the small gold knob lock and opened the pin cabinet. She lifted the pin out of the cabinet and read the small tag underneath. "Thirty-five dollars. Most of these pins are costume jewelry. When we get one with real jewels, I take it to the jeweler in Bayberry. They sell it for me on consignment."

"Sold!" Josh reached into his back pocket for his wallet. He opened it and pulled out exact change.

"Do you want me to wrap it?" Maddie asked.

"Of course," Josh said. "I'll pick it up tomorrow."

Ivy moved a wreath to fill in the space and clicked the cabinet door shut. She twisted the small key and placed it back inside a box tucked under the counter.

Josh grinned. "Just like a jewelry store."

A shadow crossed Ivy's face. "Pins are easy to steal. Mine was taken once…" her voice trailed off.

"You had a holiday pin?" Josh stepped closer to Ivy. Ivy never talked much about her past before Cranberry Bay and he never pried.

"Yes," Ivy said, her voice hardened. "It was my mom's, and I kept it tucked inside a sock bag. I always slept with it under my pillow. But one day, when I was at school, it was stolen by one of the boys living with the family."

Ivy stopped and stared into space. Her face darkened.

Josh waited, not wanting to push her if she didn't want to talk about a memory that was obviously painful.

"He was the family's biological child, and no one believed me. He needed drug money. The family didn't want to see their precious child on drugs. Keith tried to get it back for me, but the boy sold it."

"I'm sorry, Ivy." Josh placed his hand on her arm.

"I look for it," Ivy said. "When we get a pin in one of the donation boxes, I always look for it." Her voice drifted away, sad and melancholy.

Josh wanted to pull Ivy into an embrace and protect her. Was the stolen pin part of the reason she didn't like Christmas? It would be hard to have the only thing she'd kept from her mother stolen.

Max pressed against Ivy as if he knew she needed comforting. She reached down and stroked the dog's back.

"I understand if you are too busy to go to the tree farm," Josh said, understanding that Ivy's dislike of the holidays stemmed from a place much deeper than he imagined. Suzanne often competed in swim meets during the holidays, but his mom always made sure they had a Christmas, even if it didn't happen on Christmas Day. And he'd always had his grandparents, who loved him and gave him a warm, safe home at the holidays. Ivy moved around from foster home to foster home. Christmas was a charity event. Something other people bought presents for so they could feel good about the holidays.

Ivy slipped the cash into the register, the same old fashioned one Carol used. "It's no fun to pick out a tree by yourself." Her voice measured as if she was checking off another item on her to do list.

Josh walked to the door and held it open. They walked silently to his car parked in front of the antique shop. It didn't take long to drive to the Andersen Christmas Tree Farm, and the parking lot was full. Families loaded trees onto rooftops, in the back of SUVs and trucks. A large spot light illuminated a lot of already cut trees and a set of twinkle lights attached on poles surrounded it. A bonfire blazed beside a table and a couple of the Andersen's teenage sons checked people out and asked if they needed help loading cars.

A sadness overtook Josh as he gazed at the festive scene. He always picked out a tree with his grandfather, his parents were usually busy at Suzanne's December swim meets. Even when Grandpa couldn't walk the fields anymore, they'd still picked out the perfect tree in the lot.

"Are you okay?" Ivy turned to him, her voice soft and caring.

"Just thinking about Grandpa," Josh said.

Ivy nodded. "The first Christmas without people we love is hard."

Josh shook his head. "I'm sorry, Ivy. I'm being totally insensitive. This is the first Christmas without your brother."

"I miss him," Ivy said, her voice soft. "But I know he did the right thing and took on the holiday shifts for his partners so they could be home with their children."

Josh gazed at Ivy. She'd been through so much loss in her life, and yet it seemed to create a resilience in her, an ability to see life through its stormy moments. He promised Keith he would watch out for her this holiday season, but now, he wondered if she was watching out for him and his first year without his grandfather.

"Mr. Morton!"

Celia, one of the students in his class, waved at him from where she helped her dad, Kevin, load a large spruce tree onto the back of their car. He'd known Kevin since elementary school and as one of the town's public works employees, appreciated his help with the tree lighting each year.

"Let me help with that." Josh hurried over to the car and took one end of the tree. He shifted it upward with Kevin.

"She wanted a big one," Kevin lowered his voice. "I think I'm trying to make up for fact she isn't spending the holiday with her mom. It's the first year with the divorce final and her mom wanted to take a cruise." His voice hardened.

Kevin's infatuation with Kelly started in high school and she barely noticed him. After high school, Kelly left to travel down the coast in a van. She returned two weeks later, shaken and unwilling to talk about her trip. Kevin spent every moment he could with her and soon the two were engaged. But Kelly was barely home. Once she married Kevin, she found every reason to spend a weekend away. Kevin hoped it would stop after Celia would born, but it hadn't and finally, Kelly left for good and the marriage ended.

"I can't wait for the Holiday Express!" Celia jumped up and down on one foot and then the other. She lowered her voice and motioned for Josh to lean close. "Even if I know Santa Claus isn't real."

"Santa isn't real?" Josh boomed. "Of course he is!"

Celia shook her head. "No, he's not."

Ivy stepped up beside them. "Santa IS real. He's right here." Ivy pointed to the little girl's heart.

Josh grinned. Ivy's feelings toward the holidays did have a soft spot, a spot that wanted to encourage a young girl's belief in the spirit of the season.

"Celia," Kevin said. "Time to get in the car. The tree is loaded."

Celia wrapped her arms around Josh. "See you tomorrow, Mr. Morton," she said. "For the class holiday party! I baked cookies!"

Celia turned to look at Ivy. "I still don't believe in Santa."

Ivy smiled. "That's okay. Santa believes in you."

Celia grimaced and whirled away.

"You were good with her," Josh said as they walked away and toward the tree lot.

"It's hard to believe in Santa when you lose a parent."

Josh picked up Ivy's mitten hand and squeezed. "I'm sorry, Ivy." His heart contracted at the pain Ivy must have felt as a child, and how she became the strong woman he knew her to be. Even in high school, when he'd first met her, she was strong willed and determined.

Ivy looked up at him, her bright eyes glittered in the light shining down on them from the tall lights surrounding the tree lot. Josh fought the urge to kiss her lips and pull her close to him.

"Shall we pick out that tree?" Ivy asked.

Josh squeezed her hand, and keeping his hand in hers, headed toward the multiple trees leaning against the back fence.

JOSH AND IVY wrestled the tall spruce up the narrow staircase to the loft apartment above the carriage house of the tall, stately Victorian home. The home still belonged to the Davis family, but they'd converted the carriage house into a one-bedroom apartment. The space was perfect for Josh, but as they hauled the tree up the narrow staircase and into the living area, the room seemed cramped.

"I think we're going to have to move a couple pieces

of furniture." Ivy studied the coffee table and a large plush chair.

They leaned the tree against the wall, moved the coffee table to the side, and shifted the chair away from the window. Josh grabbed the tree stand he'd set out earlier, and together, they hoisted the tree into the stand. Ivy held onto the middle as Josh knelt and twisted the small turnkeys so the tree was snug in the stand.

Ivy stepped back. Her feet knocked into a stack of orange Lionel model train car boxes. The boxes crashed to the ground. "I'm sorry." She knelt beside the boxes scattered across the living room floor.

Josh knelt beside her. "It's Grandpa's Christmas train set. Mom is trying to get Dad to pack up all of Grandpa's trains, but Dad keeps unpacking them. I took these cars and hoped to set them up around my tree." He eyed the space under the tree. It seemed a lot smaller than the one at his grandfather's house.

"I'm happy to help you set it up. Two hands are better than one!"

"But the tree has to be decorated first. Otherwise, we'll step on the train."

Ivy removed her jacket and placed it across the couch. "Where are your ornaments?"

"Over there," Josh pointed at a small box on the table. His heart lifted with joy, encouraged to see Ivy wanting to stay and help with the tree.

Ivy walked over and looked in to see an odd mix match of ornaments. Some were hand crocheted. Others were the kind children once made from clay and stuck them in the oven and then painted them. She held up a yellow giraffe with black spots. "Did you make this?"

Josh grinned. "Suzanne did." He fumbled around in the box and pulled out an ornament in the shape of a brown bear. "I made this one. Mom gave me these when she redid her tree a couple years ago. She wanted it to be themed and thought I might like the childhood ornaments."

Ivy unwrapped a handsewn circle ornament with a snowflake in the center.

"Grandma made that one," Josh said. "Grandpa always hung it near the top of the tree."

"That's where it should go." Ivy stood on her tiptoes but couldn't reach the top branches.

Josh wrapped his arms around her middle and lifted her off her feet. "Here you go."

Ivy placed the ornament on the top branches and Josh slowly lowered her to the ground.

He didn't remove his hands from around her middle and held her, breathing in her soft scent. Ivy pressed back against him and didn't move. He felt her breathing deeply before she shifted slightly.

"Sorry." Josh released her and stepped away. He reached into the box as the heat raced through him. He couldn't remember the last time he felt this attracted to someone. And he couldn't let himself go there. He often wished he could be closer to Suzanne, but her swimming took her away so much of the time. Ivy was the sister he'd never found in Suzanne, except for those feelings he had after kissing her. It'd been a relief to date Kami because it made Ivy feel safer. He had a girlfriend and convinced himself Ivy was just like a sister. But now that girlfriend wall crumbled. He hadn't told anyone in Cranberry Bay about their break-up because he wasn't ready to be exposed. He couldn't risk his special friendship with Ivy, could he?

Josh picked up the angel. She was made of a round paper middle that looked like an old toilet paper roll painted gold. The head was made of a Styrofoam ball with golden ribbon as her hair. Her eyes were painted a deep jet black and seemed to have a sparkle to them.

Ivy opened a small package of tinsel. She hung a strand of tinsel on the tree. "Did you and Suzanne help with your family tree, too?"

Josh stiffened. "Not usually," he said. "I always helped Grandpa put up his tree, but Mom liked to do ours alone."

"Alone?"

Josh nodded and pulled a small ladder out of the front closet. He brought it to the tree and stepped on it with the angel in his hand. "Mom and Dad often traveled the day after Christmas to go to a swim meet. Mom liked to get the tree up and take it down with as much efficiency as she could manage. She took the tree down on Christmas night."

He placed the angel on the tree. "I helped my grandparents decorate their tree." He loved decorating the tree at his grandparents. His grandmother owned a collection of ornaments she picked up at holiday markets, traveling, and always loved the ones Josh gave her for Christmas. She made sure those hung on the front branches.

Ivy knelt beside the model train boxes. "These are the North Pole Central Passenger cars. The extension pack."

"Grandpa attended all the model train shows," Josh plunked down beside her. "These were his favorite. The only ones he set up at Christmas."

"Where do we start?" Ivy shifted a station platform to the side of the passenger car.

Josh handed her a stack of tracks that were caught together. "We start with the tracks."

AN HOUR LATER, the tracks lay in a circle around the tree and the train whooshed by with a clickety-clack. The black steam engine pulled a coach car, observation car, and combination car past a station platform.

"How about I cook us some dinner?" Josh stood. His stomach growled. It'd been hours since the school lunch. "I've got some hamburger in the refrigerator and a couple cans of chili beans. I make a mean chili."

"Sounds good to me." Ivy curled up on the sofa, and stared at the holiday lights on the tree. "The tree really came out well."

Josh smiled. She looked so comfortable sitting on the couch, her legs curled underneath her. Josh wasn't sure if he'd ever seen Ivy relaxed. He hoped that his plan of making her enjoy Christmas was working.

"Don't move," Josh said. "I'll get dinner started." He

commanded Alexa to play holiday music and the soft familiar tune of *Oh Come All Ye Faithful* filled the room.

Josh walked into the small kitchen and dropped the hamburger meat into a pot. He stirred in some onions and garlic and hummed in tune to the music in the other room. After the hamburger cooked, he added the spices and beans, set the timer for forty minutes, and turned the stove to simmer.

Josh poured a couple mugs of cider and popped each one in the microwave to warm the liquid. He walked back into the living room. Josh placed the mugs of steaming cider on the coffee table. The tree glowed and the train hummed as it went around the tree, letting out a soft whistle as it rounded the left edge of the tree.

"This is beautiful," Ivy said, her voice soft and warm.

The light caught Ivy's eyes and they sparkled. Her cheeks glowed in the light. *"You're beautiful,"* the words lingered on the tips of his tongue. Josh sank onto the couch beside her. She turned to him, and he moved closer to her. His eyes trailed over her cheeks to her lips. She licked them and leaned toward him. The heat rose inside him, and he couldn't fight it anymore. He lowered his head to hers and their lips met in a soft kiss. A kiss that flooded him with the memories of that high school kiss, and how he'd felt filled with excitement and joy. Josh deepened the kiss and Ivy's mouth parted. A soft sigh escaped. This wasn't high school Ivy. This was grown-up Ivy whose soft body called to him, tempting him for more. He ran his hands alongside her sides, and she shivered under his touch.

"Josh," Ivy whispered.

Josh wrapped his arms around her, pulling her close against him. She pressed against him and opened to him, her soft mouth opened to his as he encircled her and moved his hands, caressing her and drawing her closer to him.

Chapter 11

osh's phone buzzed from the small table beside the couch and Ivy pulled away. Kami's name flashed across his phone screen.

"I'm sorry." Ivy stood up. "This was wrong. Kami—" She turned away and slipped into her coat. Kissing Josh was the wrong thing to do. The moment caught her off guard. The sparkling tree, the smell of the hot cider, the train, all of it so comforting and luring her to what she'd always wanted, a home, someone to love at the holidays. But Josh was not that someone for her. She was not going to make the same mistake she'd made before. She was young then, naïve, but she wasn't anymore. She knew what happened when you put your heart on the line and it was whisked away with the choice of another.

"I will drive you home," Josh said. "Wait a minute." He grabbed his keys and picked up his phone. "Kami. No, Ivy, we haven't—"

"She's your girlfriend. We got carried away. It won't happen again." Ivy strode to the door and walked down the stairs to his car. He stepped around her and opened the door for her. She buckled her seat belt and stared straight ahead as he slid in next to her.

"Ivy," Josh said. "About…."

"No," Ivy shook her head. "I was helping you with your tree. That's all it is. A friend helping a friend."

"But…"

"Please," Ivy said. "Just take me home. I have a lot to do."

She crossed her legs at the ankle. She needed her checklists to protect her emotions crashing inside of her. She knew it was wrong to get swept away in the holiday spirit. It always led to bad things happening.

Josh inserted the keys into the ignition and turned on the headlights. Ivy turned her head and looked out the window. She pushed away the tears threatening to overtake her.

In minutes, Josh pulled up in front of the back of her shop and the door leading up the stairs to her apartment above the antique shop. A small plastic Santa glowed in the window. Max barked.

"Thanks for your help tonight," Josh said, his voice stiff.

"You're welcome. That's what friends do." She leaned hard into the word friend, hoping Josh would understand. They were friends and that was all. That was all they could be. Ivy grabbed her bag, slipped out of the car, and the cold air hit her cheeks.

She took a deep breath. The tears rolled down her cheeks. It was so easy to drop her guard around Josh. He'd been her friend for so long. And it was the holidays. She missed her brother and Tom and Carol. She missed the simple Christmas they always had, one gift each, and a small ham with a few sides. And always, Christmas cookies from Sasha's bakery. She'd let herself get carried away because she was missing everyone and was lonely.

But she could not do that. Josh and Kami were a couple, and an engagement was sure to be coming this Christmas. Even though Josh hadn't talked about Kami since she'd left to take the job in Seattle. It didn't matter. Josh was grieving his grandfather this first year without him. Just like her own feelings of loneliness. It'd been easy to get carried away with feelings that would vanish once the tree was taken down, the ornaments packed away, and the lights gone.

Ivy headed up the stairs and Max greeted her at the door. He barked and she slipped his leash around his collar and led him back down the set of stairs and walked to a small grassy area. When he was finished, she led him upstairs. Her stomach growled and she thought about the chili cooking on the stove and that Josh was now probably eating. Ivy opened her refrigerator and took out a box of Thai take-out she hadn't eaten a few days ago. She dumped the container on a plate and popped it into the microwave. Max jumped up on two legs and licked the counter.

"Off!" Ivy pushed him down and he looked at her

with deep, brown eyes filled with sadness at being scolded.

The microwave beeped, and she opened the door and pulled out her heated dinner. She took a bite. After two bites, Ivy set her fork down. She wasn't hungry. The best thing to do was get into bed with her iPad and clipboard. She'd work on the holiday homes spreadsheet and make sure that every home had exactly what they requested in terms of items. She could also set up a few advertisements for social media. Work would take away all the emotions racing in her. It always did.

THE NEXT MORNING, after a fitful night of sleeping, Ivy opened the shop door. One of the bulbs darkened the village homes she'd placed around the train track in the front window. She walked into her office, set her bag down, and opened a small drawer with lightbulbs. She found the right size and opened the package. Ivy strode to the window and replaced the small white bulb in the ceramic toy shop. She set it beside a ceramic tall row house and a Santa's workshop.

A few years ago, a woman dropped off five large tubs filled with ceramic village houses. Ivy kept a few of the village homes before placing the rest on the floor for sale. Village homes weren't as popular as they'd once been. Most people got tired of storing them, pulling them out and setting them up after a couple seasons. Occasionally, she'd sell one or two specific homes, like Santa's workshop or a lighted home which reminded someone of their childhood home. But most of the ceramic villages were hard to sell.

She opened a bag of polyester stuffing that she used as fake snow and placed it around the village, making sure to cover the cords and tuck the lights all the way into the houses.

From outside the picture window, Gracie waved with her red mittened hand and then pulled open the door.

"The village looks fabulous." Gracie dropped her jacket hood and shook out her hair. She wore jeans and a fleece dark blue sweatshirt over a white turtleneck. Naturally athletic, Gracie spent hours hiking the trails surrounding Cranberry Bay, often alone despite the desperate pleas of her friends to hike with someone.

"It really adds a charm to the train set." Ivy clipped a light into a three-story village Victorian home.

Gracie hefted her bag from her shoulder. "I brought the most recent sales ticket data." She frowned. "Sales aren't looking good this year."

Ivy exhaled. The last couple years, Holiday Homes tour tickets declined. People complained that the homes were the same every year, decorated the same way. Ivy tried to explain that it was hard to find people to open their homes. The Holiday Homes tour was on volunteer basis and unless someone had a recent remodel they wanted to show off, most people didn't want to open their homes at Christmas and add another thing to their full plates.

Gracie sat down at a circular table and opened her

bag. She pulled out her laptop. In a few clicks she pulled up the Holiday Homes Tour spreadsheet. "We are going to need to do something to entice these sales over the next couple days."

"How about a two-for-one sale?" Ivy said. "We could offer one ticket for free to everyone who buys one."

Gracie frowned. "I'm not sure that's going to help us. The regulars have pretty much bought their tickets. Most purchased a second one for a friend or family member already."

"Advertising," Ivy said. "We need to expand our reach beyond the coast towns. Encourage more people from Seattle and Portland to come."

"But everything in Cranberry Bay is booked," Gracie said. "We just don't have that many options. We have my inn and Rylee and Bryan's river cottages. The new bed and breakfast won't open until Valentine's Day. Unless we partner with a couple of the hotels over in Seashore Cove. But they usually have their own off-season specials."

"I'll make a few calls," Ivy said. "In fact, I'll drive over to Seashore Cove this afternoon." She needed to purchase gifts for her friends, and it'd be a great afternoon of working through more of her list.

"This afternoon is the annual Soups for Santa," Gracie said. "You don't want to miss that!"

Ivy flushed. She *did* want to miss Soups for Santa. Especially today. Soups for Santa started from the high school leadership team. She worked with Josh on the event. After Josh graduated, he expanded the program to include the fire truck driving through town with its lights flashing. People came to their doors with bags of canned goods which were donated to the local food bank. Ivy enjoyed sorting the donations at the fire station. She loved organizing types of canned goods and placing them in the large boxes to take to the food bank. But that was before her kiss with Josh last night.

Gracie peered at her. "What's going on?"

"Nothing." Ivy turned away from Gracie.

"I heard you helped Josh with his tree," Gracie said. "I was at the bakery this morning and bumped into Celia and Kevin. Celia couldn't stop talking about how she saw Mr. Morton and his new girlfriend."

Ivy's face flamed. "Small towns."

Gracie leaned closer to Ivy. "You *were* the new girlfriend Celia was talking about? Did something happen?"

"I am not the new girlfriend," Ivy said, her cheeks flushed.

"You didn't answer my other question," Gracie said. "Did something happen?"

"We kissed," Ivy said, her voice low.

Gracie grabbed Ivy by the arm. "You and Josh kissed?"

"We didn't mean for it to happen," Ivy said. "We were setting up his tree and it was so warm and cozy. I just forgot myself." She turned away from Gracie.

"And there wasn't even any mistletoe," Gracie said, and smiled.

Ivy's face darkened at the memory of the high school mistletoe. That was a memory she wanted to forget.

Max nudged himself next to Ivy. He dropped a chewed up stocking.

"Max!" Ivy exclaimed. The stocking came from Mary Beth's section, the red tag with Mary Beth's name still on it.

Ivy flipped the tag over. Thirty-five dollars. She shook her head. "This is why nothing is selling in the antique shop." No one wanted to pay thirty-five dollars for a stocking when they could go up to Seaview Point and buy one for seven dollars at one of the big box shops.

Ivy stood. A trail of torn paper lay down the store aisle leading to Mary Beth's station.

"What else did you get into?" Ivy followed the trail of paper and stood in the middle of Mary Beth's area. Max had knocked over a table with Christmas sheet music and torn most of it apart. A doll lay in pieces, the stuffing from her head scattered on the floor.

Gracie's boot heels clicked on the wood floor, and she stared at the mess. "Oh my, Max!"

"I've got to get him something to keep him occupied."

"Frozen peanut butter in a Kong toy always worked for my dog." Gracie owned a Westie who was five. Callie greeted every guest at the River Rock Inn and slept in a plush pink dog bed by the front counter. Gracie loved taking her on walks at the local beaches and parks.

"I need to get back to the Inn," Gracie said. "We've got a couple rooms turning over today. She stood, pulled on her coat, and slipped her laptop back into her bag. "I'll see you at Soups for Santa."

Ivy sighed. She'd have to go to Soups for Santa. She wasn't going to be able to avoid Josh. Her friends knew she didn't enjoy attending the tree lighting, and all of them understood her reasons. But they were not going to let her hide from Josh for the rest of the holiday season in Cranberry Bay.

Ivy took a quick survey of the store. No one had come in this morning, which didn't surprise her. The wind was gusting and the last time she checked, the wind advisories and high surf warnings were up. It wasn't unusual for this time of the year to have wind and rain with high surf. Cranberry Bay was tucked away from the brunt of the ocean storms, but they could still get wind gusts and heavy rains that flooded the streets. Maybe it wasn't a good day to go to Seashore Cove and find presents for her friends. But it'd be fine to run next door and buy Max a toy or two or three.

Ivy glanced at the back door which led into Paige's shop. It'd be so easy to open it from her side and walk next door, the way she'd always visit Katie, especially on days like this. But if she opened it now, then the door would become a pass-through again. And knowing Paige, she'd probably want all her customers to use it with their dogs! No. It was best to go out the front door, into the rain and then into Paige's shop. Ivy headed to the door, flipped the sign to be back in five minutes, shut it behind her, and dashed toward the lighted store. She stayed close under the awning so she didn't get too wet. When she opened the door, Maddie stood at the counter, checking out a woman with a huge stack of toys and bones and a dog stocking.

Maddie flushed. "Ivy!"

The woman handed Maddie a credit card and without looking at Ivy, Maddie quickly ran the card while Lars bagged her items. She returned the card, stuffed a few sample treats into the bag and thanked the customer. Ivy wandered into the aisle with the toys and picked out three Kong toys, a large reindeer stuffed animal, and a bag of chew bones. She couldn't blame Maddie for wanting to work in a store where she'd have something to do more than run to the post office and mail packages. Maddie was a bright, charming teenager and she shone in a shop that allowed her to demonstrate her personable skills. She also suspected Lars was a big part of why Maddie wanted to work for Paige.

Ivy walked to the counter and set her items down. Maddie was bright red as Lars reached for a handful of sample treats and placed them beside Ivy's purchases.

"Are you feeling better?" Ivy asked and smiled at Maddie to let her know she wasn't upset. Maddie texted her last night she didn't feel well and couldn't come in to work but it looked like she caught a case of the Christmas Crush Bug and not the flu bug.

"I started feeling better," Maddie said, her ears pink. "And Paige needed the extra help. She is going to train me as an assistant with the dog classes. I'll make four dollars more than I'm making now."

"That's great," Ivy said, happy for Maddie. She couldn't pay Maddie that much to run errands for her shop, and working as an assistant in the dog classes would give Maddie another skill to add to her resume.

"I know I said I wanted to work for you," Maddie said. "But this just seemed like too good of an opportunity."

"It's business," Ivy said. "Sometimes we must go where the benefits are a little more enticing and we can gain new skills. I understand."

"Thanks, Ivy!" Maddie said and grinned at her. "I'll share my friends and family discount with you and Max."

Paige walked out of the back training room alongside a woman with a large yellow lab. "That's right. Keep him on the leash next to you. Don't let him pull too far ahead of you."

The woman followed Paige's advice and the dog walked beside her.

Ivy wished Max would do as well on his leash. It was a constant tug of war. Max pulled on his leash, he chewed on his leash, and he raced ahead of her.

Paige unhooked a flyer from the front bulletin board. "I've got a new class starting next week. It's the first class in the series to train the dogs for the reading therapy program."

"We will sign up. We have heard so much about the program and how the dogs help children feel more confident with their reading."

Paige ran her hand over the dog's back. "He'll make a good therapy dog. Labs are calm and train easily."

The woman thanked Paige at the same time Max

barked. Three loud booming barks drifted through the wall between the two shops.

"I better go," Ivy said to Maddie, taking the bag. "Max is probably tearing up the shop." She'd placed Max in the office and shut the door. She kept a clean and tidy desk and there wasn't too much to get into, but now she worried.

"There's a basic obedience class coming up in January." Paige handed Ivy a flyer. "I'd love to work with you and Max."

Ivy tightened her lips and nodded.

"I'll check my calendar." Ivy took the flyer and stuffed it in her bag. She hurried out the door and toward her shop. She could manage Max with a few frozen peanut butter toys and some practice. She didn't need training classes with Paige. Paige wanted to take over everything in Cranberry Bay. But Ivy wasn't going to allow her to train her dog, too.

She bit her lower lip. She did want to learn more about the reading dog program, not for Max, but for herself. But maybe she could practice with Max. She could read books to him and give him the toy with peanut butter. It couldn't be that hard to read out loud to a dog, especially her own dog.

Chapter 12

Josh shifted the box of canned soup to make room for more. He took another look at his watch. Where was Ivy? His stomach sunk. He knew as soon as he looked at his phone and saw Kami's name flash across that Ivy saw it, too. He hadn't heard from Kami since Halloween, and when he listened to her message, it sounded like she had too much to drink, felt lonely, and called him. He hadn't called or texted her back and she hadn't tried again. He wanted to tell Ivy. But she'd been upset and he didn't blame her. She deserved a man who could give her his whole heart.

"Everything okay?" Adam tapped his shoulder.

"Of course." Josh hefted another box of canned goods from the stack piling up where they were being sorted and placed it beside the first.

"You have checked that watch at least ten times in the last five minutes."

Josh flushed. "Just want to make sure we're running

smoothly. Seems like a lot more donations this year." The annual drive through the town brought in boxes and bags of canned goods. The Cranberry Bay residents embraced this holiday tradition with open hearts every year.

Plus, the donations from the Cranberry Bay schools also kept up with a record pace. Each class competed against others in the building. Josh's class came in second this year by only two cans of food and his class had not been happy. But although they didn't get the pizza party the first-place winners earned, they were allowed to go first to lunch for a week which gave them prize spots in line as well as the first to finish lunch and head to recess. He reminded his class the importance of acting like winners, no matter where they placed in a competition.

A woman walked in carrying a large box of canned goods. She wore long black boots over dark jeans, but he couldn't see the rest of her. Josh strode forward to take the box from her hands. When he lifted the box out of the way, he stared into Ivy's blue eyes.

"Glad you made it," he said, hoping his voice didn't betray all the emotions crashing through him. Josh couldn't imagine doing Soups for Santa without Ivy. For the last twelve years, Soups for Santa stocked the food bank shelves not only in Cranberry Bay but also Seaview Cove. It'd been during their project in high school when he realized how much he enjoyed her companionship, working side-by-side with him, not just as Keith's little sister but as a girl he admired.

"Mr. Morton!" Celia said, her voice carrying from the

open garage door of the fire station. "We've got all the school's cans in the back of the truck!"

Josh strolled across the room to the garage door where Celia and Kevin stood beside the open door of their truck. "I think we've got everything. Anne helped us load up. It sure seems like a lot this year." Kevin adjusted his Mariners ball cap.

"The classes really worked hard! A little friendly competition always helps," Josh said. Each day, kids brought in more cans. He heard a couple of them mention babysitting money and lawn mowing money they used to purchase more cans.

Adam rolled the roller cart to the open truck bed. Bryan hustled behind him and hoisted himself into the truck. He grabbed a box and handed it to Adam, who placed it on the roller cart.

Celia bounced on one foot and then the other. Her dark brown hair swung behind her. She wore a festive green sweater with an elf on the front, ripped-at-the-knee blue jeans, and tennis shoes. "I wanted to recount the cans. But Mrs. Anne wouldn't let me."

"The other second-grade class won by three cans," Josh said. "The teachers counted both our class and their class cans three times. It was always the same."

Celia crossed her hands over her chest. "I think the counting was rigged."

A red truck with blaring rock music pulled in, and Lars jumped out of the passenger side. He wore an elf hat which bounced on his head. His blond curly hair framed his face. Maddie popped out of the truck, and a boy Josh didn't recognize got out of the driver's side.

"We've got the junior class cans," Lars said. "Freshman, sophomore, and seniors are behind us."

"We're going to need all hands on deck." Josh turned around and poked his head into the fire station. "Got lots of cans here!"

Ivy, Rylee, and Gracie hurried out to the waiting truck as two white vans pulled in. "Let's set up a chain," Ivy said. "We'll spread out and pass the boxes and bags to the stack by the wall."

Josh positioned himself alongside Ivy. He reached into his jacket and pulled out his red velvet Santa cap. Turning to Ivy, he placed it on her head, his hands lingering beside her cheeks for a minute longer than he needed.

Ivy flushed. But before he could say anything, Rylee nudged him with a box. "Here you go."

Josh took the box and turned to Ivy. His fingers brushed against hers as she took the box from him. He didn't have time to think about her touch as another box came at him from Rylee. Soon, a pile grew at the end of the fire station garage wall. Every time he passed the next box to Ivy, her fingers brushed against his, but neither of them said a word.

A few more trucks and vans pulled up with boxes collected at the middle school as well as from the other classes of the high school. It took the good part of an hour for all the boxes to be unloaded and as each truck pulled in, more people joined the human line, passing boxes from hand to hand.

"That's it!" Adam said as the last van pulled away. "We got them all!"

Stacks of boxes were piled alongside the back corner of the fire station. The boxes would be sorted and distributed throughout the food banks of the small towns along the coast. It was enough that the food banks would have plenty for the winter months.

"Soups on!" Sawyer stepped out of the fire station. He wore a white chef's hat and an apron dotted with small Santas over his clothes. "Everyone, help yourself. We've got chicken noodle and broccoli cheddar.

"And a lot of homemade rolls!" Sasha called from the open door.

Josh walked beside Ivy into the fire station. He grinned at Sawyer. Sawyer never would have worn an apron like that until he fell in love with Katie. Josh watched both Sawyer and Bryan soften and lean into the women who loved them, becoming more flexible and forgiving, not holding the world in such a rigid stance. He admired what love looked like in his friends' lives. He knew surrendering to love was a challenge for both. And although he cared about her, Josh admitted he'd never felt that way about Kami. There was a part of himself he'd always kept closed off from her.

The gas fireplace glowed in the corner of the room, festive holiday decorations strung from the doorway, and stockings with each of the Cranberry Bay firefighter's names hung on the mantel. The long tables were pushed together to form one big table in the middle of the room. Katie, Sawyer, and Sasha stood behind one table filled with fresh rolls, three pots of soup, bottles of water, and soda. Katie wore a matching apron to Sawyer's, and she wiped her hands on it. Sawyer leaned over and wiped a smudge of broccoli cheddar from her nose. She giggled like a school-girl. Josh wanted what the two of them had. He wanted what Bryan and Rylee had. But why did it have to be so hard to get where he would allow himself to surrender to love?

"Ivy! Josh!" Sawyer waved them to the front of the line. "You two go first!"

Josh followed Ivy to the front of the line. She walked with her back straight and rigid ahead of him, as if all her emotions were bottled up inside and if she made one move in the wrong direction, everything would spill out. He wanted to see her enjoy the Christmas holiday, and she'd been warming up, but then he'd ruined it with allowing himself to get swept away and kissing her.

"After you," he motioned for Ivy to go ahead of him.

She took a blue ceramic bowl and selected the chicken noodle soup. Katie ladled a large scoop full on her plate and Sasha plopped a roll beside the bowl. Josh pointed to the broccoli cheddar and Sawyer dumped a heaping scoop in his bowl.

He followed Ivy to the long table and pulled out a chair beside her.

The rest of the group settled into their places with steaming soup bowls and buttered bread.

"Here's to another successful Soups for Santa!" Bryan raised his glass.

Cheers went around the table.

Ivy blushed.

Without thinking, Josh placed his hand on hers. She quietly slipped it away and dropped it under the table.

Adam tapped him on the shoulder. He raised an eyebrow and nodded toward Ivy, who turned away from Josh and chatted with Tyler, sitting on the other side of her.

Josh shook his head. Ivy had made up her mind about him and he didn't blame her for feeling that way. She deserved a man who could surrender to his feelings for her.

Chapter 13

"I'm sorry, Ivy," Sasha brushed her floured hands on the red gingham apron. "I just can't take another order. I'm swamped with holiday pies, and you know how it's been trying to get help right now."

Ivy grimaced. She understood about the worker shortage. Maddie working for Paige meant all the orders coming into her online shops were left to be filled by her. She'd been hustling the last couple days to get the orders filled, packaged up, and taken to the post office.

"What about Katie pitching in to help make the cookies for the Holiday Homes tour?" Sasha tossed a stick of butter into the blender. She didn't consult the recipe book, open beside her for measurements.

Ivy shook her head. "Katie has her hands full with getting the barn ready to be Santa's Workshop for the Holiday Express."

"Gracie?" Sasha measured half a cup of sugar.

"She has choir practice every night for the community church Christmas service." Gracie played the piano every year at the Christmas service. She started practicing her holiday songs months ago in July. It was the highlight of her holiday season.

"Not Rylee." Sasha shook her head and turned on the blender.

Ivy grinned. Both of them remembered the year Rylee cooked Thanksgiving and invited everyone over. The turkey wasn't done until ten p.m., the potatoes were hard as rocks and cold, and the pies were mushy in the middle.

"I'll see if I can find some old recipes in cookbooks in one of the vendors stalls." How hard could holiday cookies be to make?

A woman rang the small bell on the countertop. "Hello! I'd like to order a sandwich!"

Sasha turned off the blender and rolled her eyes at Ivy. "Aren't holidays fun? Everyone needs something now."

She turned and walked to the counter. Ivy slipped out the back door of the bakery and walked a block down the alley to the backdoor of the antique shop. She inserted her key into the lock and opened the door. She headed down the aisle and toward Mary Beth's area. Mary Beth always displayed books. She'd have a couple recipes for holiday cooking. It'd be easy to take a few photos of a couple recipes and then follow the directions.

On a green shelf, a small collection of silver cookie cutters hung from red ribbon. Ivy unhooked a Santa, a reindeer, and a star. A basket of children's *Little Golden*

Books sat beside a sleigh, and a pair of ice skates tied to the top of the sleigh. But there weren't any holiday cookbooks.

She wasn't worried. One of the vendors was bound to have a cookie book. Ivy worked her way through the booths. She uncovered quite a few other cookbooks including one about barbeque, one for soups, and one for pizzas. But there were no holiday baking books.

Ivy's heart raced a bit faster. Gracie and Katie always made the holiday cookies for the Holiday Homes tour, and it wasn't something she worried about, until now. Ivy peered out the window toward the library. The town's small library wasn't open until eleven since Mrs. Shuster retired, the library was staffed with volunteers until they could find someone to hire full-time. The library windows were dark and the lights out.

The panic rose in Ivy's chest. "Don't panic," she told herself. "You have the internet at your fingertips." She taught herself to sew using videos from the internet, she could teach herself how to make holiday cookies.

Ivy strode into her office and clicked into her computer. She Googled Christmas cookies and pages of pages of recipes came up.

"See," she said to herself. "Look at this."

Max nosed her hand. The peanut butter toys kept him busy, and when he didn't get much of a response from her, he settled back into his dog bed and continued licking at his toy.

Ivy clicked on the first link. Little green trees clustered on a festive holiday plate. That couldn't be too hard. Ivy read the recipe for Spritz cookies. It seemed easy but she didn't have a cookie press to make the tree shapes.

"Okay," she said to herself. "Just find a different recipe."

Ivy scrolled down to the next recipe. "Cut out sugar cookies." She looked at the Santa and tree in her hand. She'd roll up a batch of dough. She'd seen a couple of rolling pins in the vendor's booths. She'd purchase one.

Ivy read through the recipe. Minutes later, she leaned back in her chair and exhaled. What was she thinking? She didn't have the kitchen tools for any of the cookies. She didn't bake and she rarely cooked. She didn't own a stand or handheld mixer. She ran through her friends and their kitchens. Rylee didn't own much in terms of baking tools. Bryan enjoyed cooking, but Ivy couldn't remember breads or cookies ever coming out of Rylee's kitchen. Sasha needed hers at the bakery for the holiday rush. Katie needed hers for cookie baking with Lauren. Gracie used hers for baking the scones and muffins she served each morning at the inn. She didn't want to add to any of her friends already too full holiday plates by asking to borrow their kitchens for a few hours, especially when she didn't really know how to bake holiday cookies.

The door to her shop chimed and Josh's voice rang out. "Hello! Ivy!"

Ivy stood up and walked into the store. Josh wasn't the best option, considering her feelings for him and what happened when they decorated his tree, but right now he was the only option she had.

"What's wrong?" Josh hurried over to her. "Did something happen?"

Tears pooled in the corners of Ivy's eyes, and she pushed them away. She didn't need to cry. It was just cookies. But she knew it wasn't just cookies. It was everything pilling up on her. The shop wasn't doing well this season, Keith wasn't home, the Holiday Homes Tour was flirting with a disastrous year in terms of ticket sales. Christmas had always been a struggle and this year it just felt like everything was against her. Her well-kept lists were not keeping her protected against the onslaught of Christmas misery.

"Hey." Josh tossed his arm around her and pulled her close. She leaned against his soft sweater and inhaled his strong spicey scent. "It's going to be okay. Whatever it is." His voice was deep and soothing as he held her.

"Do you know how to bake Christmas cookies?" Ivy mumbled against his chest.

"What?" Josh stepped away and looked down at Ivy. Protectiveness softened his face.

"I have to bake the cookies for the Holiday Homes Tour. I have these cookie cutters and recipes," Ivy waved her hand toward her office and the open computer with recipes. "But I don't have the right kitchen things. And I've never made Christmas cookies."

Josh gazed down at Ivy. "You've never made Christmas cookies?" His eyes sparkled.

"No," Ivy shook her head, wiping away her tears. "Carol always got the store-bought kind. She didn't like to bake."

"But the Holiday Homes Tour always serves cookies. You didn't make them?"

"Katie made them," Ivy said. "Lauren loves to help Katie make Christmas cookies. But this year, they are working on getting the farm ready for the Holiday Express."

"I love making cookies," Josh said, his eyes twinkled with delight. "It was something I always did with Grandma. I could find her recipes. I'm pretty sure they are at Mom's. Mom isn't much of a Christmas cookie baker, but she's made a few of Grandma's recipes over the years."

Josh pulled out his phone and texted Beth Morton. *Do you still have Grandma's recipe for holiday cookies?*

Immediately, Beth texted back. *Of course.*

Can Ivy and I come over and get it? We need to make cookies for the Holiday Homes Tour.

Why don't you use my kitchen? Beth asked. *Suzanne and I are going out.*

Would love that, Josh texted. *Thanks.*

"Problem solved," Josh pocked his phone. "Mom has the recipe, and we can use her kitchen."

"I'll close the shop for a few hours," Ivy said. "This rain is keeping people away. And I don't think I'm going to miss many sales this morning."

Ivy strode to the door and flipped the sign to closed. She turned, and Josh stood with Max's leash in his hands. "Max wants to help, too," he said.

Ivy picked up Max's Kong. "Do you have peanut butter?"

Josh threw back his head and laughed. The sound filled the store and Ivy's heart lifted. It was all going to be okay. She felt her stomach settle and the warm feeling inside her, the same feeling her friendship with Josh always gave her, safety, security, and comfort.

———

THIRTY MINUTES LATER, after a quick stop to the store to get butter, flour, and sugar, Josh pulled out rolling pins, pastry cloths, flour, sugar, and a bag of cookie cutters that was big enough to fill an entire drawer.

"I've never seen so many cookie cutters." Ivy opened the bag and pulled out three different sizes of metal circles. "What are these for?"

"Wreaths." Josh peered over her shoulder and his eyes widened. "I guess we do have a lot. Grandma never got rid of anything, and it looks like Mom combined her cookie cutters with Grandma's."

"Josh?" Beth stepped into the kitchen. She wore dark denim blue jeans, a periwinkle sweater, and red Santa hats dangled from her ears. "Suzanne and I are going to drive over to Seashore Cove and do a little shopping and have lunch. Do you need anything?"

"Not that I can think of," Josh said. "I've pretty much wrapped up Christmas."

"Thank you for letting us use your kitchen," Ivy said. "I really didn't know what I was going to do about the Holiday Homes Tour cookies."

"Of course, dear," Beth said. "We've all shifted things

around this year. Losing Daniel left a lot of spaces in the holiday season." She swallowed and blinked rapidly.

Josh stepped over and touched his mom on the shoulder. "It's hard this year. But we'll get through it."

Beth looked up at Josh, and her eyes brightened.

Ivy swallowed. Josh protected and took care of everyone in his life. He recognized when people were hurting, and he knew just the right thing to say to make it better.

Beth picked up a large, over-the-shoulder purse as Suzanne honked the car horn. "Better go!" She hurried out the back kitchen door.

Josh reached for three small pegs behind the door and grabbed two aprons. "Ready?"

Ivy took the apron from Josh. It was one of Katie's with small gingerbread men dancing across the front and matched the one Josh slipped on.

"We'll start with this one." Josh flipped through a brown index box and pulled out a worn handwritten recipe. "Then, while that dough is chilling, we'll work on the gingerbread men, do a batch of spritz, and circle back to the cut-outs. Those will take the longest because we'll have to decorate them after they cook."

Ivy felt comforted by Josh's easy take-charge stance, and she understood how his young students loved him and felt safe and protected. There was something in his gentle, easy-going manner that took all her fears and worries and tossed them away.

Josh guided her in how to cream the butter and sugar while he mixed the dry ingredients in a bowl. When the butter was creamed, sugars and egg added, Josh carefully added the flour mixture and then directed her to stir. In minutes, rolls of dough were chilling in the refrigerator and the gingerbread recipe was underway.

It didn't take Ivy long to catch on to the fact that most of the cookie dough consisted of sugars, butter, and eggs, mixed until creamy. In a separate bowl, she combined flour and baking powder tossed in. She was fascinated by the spritz cookies and the cookie press and marveled at the small trees that emerged from each press.

Soon, the kitchen smelled like Sasha's bakery. She and Josh worked steadily to cut out gingerbread men, cookie press trees, and slide cookie trays in and out of the oven. A steady line of cookies filled the counter on parchment paper.

Josh hummed holiday tunes and Ivy found herself singing alongside him as they baked.

"And now, the cut outs!" Josh pulled out the first two rolls of chilled dough from the refrigerator. He plunked them down in front of Ivy and dug through the bag of cut-outs. His eyes sparkled, and a dab of flour dotted his nose. Without thinking about it, Ivy leaned over to wipe the flour off his nose. He reached up and took her hand. For a minute, he held it and neither of them said anything. She gazed into his dark eyes, which pooled with something deep, something that wanted to pull her in and never let go.

Josh leaned forward, his eyes meeting hers.

She leaned closer to him as the back door opened.

"It smells great in here!" Suzanne called.

Quickly, Ivy pulled away. She plunked a silver Santa into the dough.

"I'm sorry," Suzanne said. "I was interrupting a little holiday magic." She giggled.

Ivy didn't look up at either Josh or Suzanne.

"You're back early." Josh's voice sounded strained.

"Mom and I are going to lunch at Sasha's. We wanted to check to see if the two of you wanted anything?"

"Sasha makes great turkey sandwiches." Ivy placed a cookie cutter into the dough and pressed firmly.

"Yes," Josh said. "How about two turkey sandwiches?"

"Two turkey sandwiches coming up! You two be careful of that Christmas magic." She laughed and slipped out the door.

"Josh," Ivy said, and paused. Was it really her place to say something about Suzanne? Today, she seemed happy, the dark circles under her eyes faded and her voice bright and cheerful. Maybe whatever it was that bothered her had worked out.

"Mmm." Josh placed one of the cut-outs on a cookie tray.

"Is everything okay with Suzanne?" The words fell out of Ivy's mouth. She had to say something. If something was wrong with Keith and she didn't notice, she'd want someone to point it out to her.

"I think so," Josh frowned. "Why do you ask?"

Ivy pressed down on the cookie cutter, and kept her eyes averted from Josh. "She came to the sewing circle lazy pant sewing day last week and just seemed sad or upset about something."

Josh cut around a dough Santa with a small knife. "I know what you mean," he said. "I guess I didn't want to really see it. She has seemed sad, distracted, since she's been home. She doesn't talk about her swim team at all."

"Maybe you can—"

"Talk to her," Josh snapped his fingers. "Of course. I'm just sorry I didn't see anything sooner."

"I didn't want to interfere," Ivy said. "You've never interfered with Keith and I."

"You would never interfere," Josh stopped and looked up at Ivy. His eyes met hers and compassion flooded them. "I appreciate that you said something."

Ivy lifted the cookie cutter. A perfectly formed Santa lay on the cloth in the dough. She frowned. Was she supposed to cut around the dough to lift it to the cookie sheet?

"Let me show you." Josh stepped around her and cut a couple more shapes into the dough. He pressed hard and the dough lifted with the cutter. "If you press hard enough, the dough will lift right with the cutter and then you just tap it on the cookie sheet, and it will fall right off." Josh tapped the cookie cutter against the sheet. A tree dropped onto the sheet.

"I see!" Ivy picked up a star and pressed it into the dough, hard. She lifted the cookie cutter, and the star came with it. She tapped the cutter on the cookie sheet and a star lay beside Josh's tree.

"I never thanked you for finding the tree topper," Josh said, his voice deep. "You really helped me out."

"That's what friends do." Ivy hoped her voice didn't betray her. She felt much more for Josh than friendship.

"Yes," Josh said. "That is what friends do." The words lingered between them, settling into the cookies. Friends. She and Josh were friends. Even if the air between them sizzled with something far bigger, they were friends. And that was what mattered. That was the important thing.

Chapter 14

J osh lifted the tray of wrapped cookies from the backseat of his car. Rain pelted him. Freezing rain. The small temperature gauge tucked into an empty flowerpot in front of Ivy's shop read thirty-three degrees. The weather forecast said there could be a chance of an ice storm today. It wasn't common for Cranberry Bay to have ice storms. the warm ocean air usually kept the temperature from dropping to freezing. The same was true for snowstorms. But that didn't mean an ice or snowstorm couldn't happen occasionally.

Josh remembered a big snowstorm during elementary school. The power was out for days. It wasn't like a snow-storm where everyone could get outside. The storm started with an ice storm. The ice cracked trees, broke power lines, and made a general mess of the town. But everyone banded together. The homes with generators offered hot showers and meals. The fire department made their rounds, checking on everyone in town, making sure the elderly and young children were in a warm place. And in the spring new trees were planted to replace the ones which split from the heavy ice and snow. Cranberry Bay residents supported each other.

Josh carried the tray of cookies to the front of the Red Door Antique shop. Ivy stood in the doorway, hands on her hips as she glared daggers at Paige. Unaware that Ivy looked like she could strangle her, Paige hung a blue ribbon onto the dog bone wreath on her door.

"It's starting to sleet." Ivy pointed to the sleeting rain running down the side of the building. "The ribbon is going to get ruined."

"You're right, thanks!" Paige unhooked the ribbon. "I'm just so excited to be a first-place winner of the contest my first year!"

A woman with a three-legged dog ducked under the awnings. "Pebble," she said to the dog. "Over here!"

The dog walked over to the treat basket Paige held out. "It's sure a nasty morning." The woman pulled her hood tighter around her head. She wore black boots, a winter coat, and a scarf draped around her neck. "I had tickets for the Holiday Homes Tour, but I don't think I want to risk being out with this storm. I'm staying at the charming inn over there," she pointed to Gracie's River Rock Inn. "I think I'll just go back and sit by the fireplace!"

"We've got cookies." Josh held out the tray. "Home-made! You don't want to miss the Holiday Homes Tour!"

"The cookies look great. I'll take a few to go, but I'm not going to risk walking around town with this sleet coming down." The woman took two cookies and with her dog, headed back toward the inn.

Josh shrugged and walked into the antique shop behind Ivy. The lights above their heads flickered.

"Oh no," Ivy looked up at the flickering lights. "If the power goes out, we can't have the tour! No one is going to want people walking through homes that are half-lit or dark rooms."

Josh didn't want to mention that if the rain/sleet mix continued, the Holiday Homes Tour wouldn't be a hit either. The owners wouldn't take the liability risk of people coming up steps and sidewalks that were icy, even with salt on them.

"It'll stop soon," he said. "We just have to wait it out!" Josh wanted Ivy to catch the magic of the spirit of the holiday. He knew the kiss at his house dampened things for her but he wanted to bring back the sparkle in her eye and what he knew to be holiday magic.

Ever since he was a child, he watched the holiday magic at his grandparent's home. *"There is a certain thing that happens,"* his grandmother used to say. *"But you have to watch for it. It's there, every Christmas."*

Josh saw that magic. He'd seen it in his students when they were unexpectedly given a holiday meal. He'd seen it in the staff he worked with as surprise gifts that showed up on teachers' desks from those students least expected to give a gift. And he'd always seen the holiday magic in each child's eyes as they boarded the Holiday Express.

But Josh never saw Ivy with the holiday magic. He watched her work with multiple checklists, her absence at the tree lighting ceremony each year, and the relief on her face when January rolled around and the season's decorations were tucked away. He wanted this year to be different for her. And a canceled Holiday Homes Tour was not the way to bring magic to the season.

Rain sleeted at the windows. "People should be here." Ivy drummed her fingers on the counter. "It's eleven o'clock, and except for the woman in Paige's shop, no one has come to pick up their tickets."

"The tour goes until four," Josh said. "People still have time." He wanted to reassure Ivy and take away the look in her eyes.

Ivy's cell phone buzzed, and she picked it up. "Yes, I totally understand. Yes, yes. I will take your home off the tour." She hung up, pressed a button and played back two messages. Both were canceling their homes on the tour due to the possibility of slick sidewalks and walkways.

"That's three homes canceled." Ivy's voice rang with despair. "People just don't want the liability."

Josh understood the homeowner's feelings. It snowed so rarely in Cranberry Bay, and they didn't have snowplows or put down salt on the roads. People just waited for the storms to pass.

"How many homes are on the tour?" Josh asked.

"We started with five," Ivy said. "Usually we have seven, but we just weren't able to get as many this year. And now we are down to two. We can't run the tour with two homes."

"Mmm…. Let me see what I can do." Josh pulled out

his cell phone and punched in Anne's phone number. She answered on the first ring.

"We've got a problem," Josh said. "People are canceling the holiday homes for the tour. Any chance we can use the school? The classroom doors are decorated. Many of the classrooms have student work hung and lights around bulletin boards. People will love getting a peak into the insides of the historic elementary school."

"Of course!" Anne said. "I don't know if it will be very warm because I can't get the heat up that fast but add the school to the tour. I'll get over there and open the rooms. We'll get some sand down in the walkways just in case it gets a little icy."

Josh hung up the phone. "That's one more," he grinned at Ivy as he hit his Mom's name on his phone.

Beth answered on the first ring.

"Mom," Josh said. "I need a favor." Before Josh could finish explaining the situation, Beth told him to add her home to the tour.

"I've got some sand in the garage," Beth said.

"I'll pop by and get it onto the steps and sidewalk." Josh clicked his phone to off.

"That's two," Josh tapped the paper in front of Ivy. "Can we make up a sheet to tuck into the map? I can give some history on Mom's house and the school to write up."

"Of course. I'll call Gracie. She wrote the descriptions and did the map. I'll have her make an insert page and bring it over. We'll make some copies and stick them into the maps."

"I think the temperature is rising!" Paige entered the antique shop. "These came in yesterday. I just unburied them under all the dog food bags." She held out a package of Kongs. "I thought you might like a couple for Max."

"Thanks," Ivy took the toys from Paige.

"I just got a call from Mrs. Westin, and she told me she canceled her home on the tour," Paige said. "I'd like to offer mine. It's nothing fancy. But I want to help."

"That's really generous of you," Josh said. "People are going to love being able to see inside your home. It's never been on the tour."

Paige beamed. "It's a darling cottage. I was lucky to be able to buy it. Bryan let me know as soon as it came on the market, and I put in the offer. Full price and a little more!"

"Okay," Ivy nodded. "I'll add yours to the list. I'll let Gracie know."

"Before you do that," Josh paused. "There's one more I want to add."

"Who?" Ivy asked.

"Mine," Josh said. He blushed, and his voice dropped. "I know it's small and it isn't decorated the way the other homes are, but the train is there and the tree." He stopped, remembering setting up the tree and the train with Ivy.

She flushed looking at him, and he knew she was remembering, too. "Thank you," she said, her voice softened.

"That's the magic of Christmas." Josh stepped close

to her. A spot of sunshine appeared through the clouds outside and moved across Ivy's face, giving her a glow that could only be described one way—the magic of Christmas.

The door chimed, and three women walked in. "We're here to pick up our Holiday Homes tour tickets."

"We've had some new additions," Ivy said. "We're just getting the maps ready. Would you like a cookie and to browse the store?"

Josh slid the plate of cookies toward the ladies.

"What a charming idea." One woman picked up a Spritz tree. "I haven't enjoyed one of these in ages." She took a bite. "Mmmm...Just as I remembered."

"Look!" The second woman called as she stood by Mary Beth's pair of ice skates and sled. "Wouldn't this look just darling by my front door?"

"What a charming store and town," the third woman said. "I can't wait to look around while we wait for the maps."

Josh turned and grinned at Ivy.

Her eyes sparkled.

Chapter 15

"It was a fabulous tour! The school building was so fun to see!"

"And the darling apartment with the trains! My husband loved the pictures I texted him!"

Ivy smiled at the chatter in the antique shop as she wrapped another box of vintage ornaments in red tissue paper. Not only had the Holiday Homes Tour been one of the most successful, despite the late start due to the icy temperature, but all afternoon, people streamed into the Red Door Antiques to buy items to add to their holiday décor and for gifts. Ivy was pretty sure most of the vendors sold out of most of their holiday decor. Peter Johnson's booth even sold a fair number of items, including old car license plates, glass fishing floats, and various vintage tools. A few of the customers confessed they weren't sure what the tools were used for, but when snapping a photo and texting it to a friend or family member, all were told to buy the item immediately and it was rare to find one in such good condition.

At six o'clock, after the last customer left, Ivy walked over to the front door and flipped the sign to closed. She breathed a sigh of relief. The Holiday Homes Tour would be able to help fund the Holiday Express and she would be able to tell her vendors their annual vendor fee could stay the same this year without any new hikes to prices. And, she switched the front window train switch to off, it was all thanks to Josh's quick thinking and the addition of the new homes and the school.

Mid-way through the tour, Anne Marks texted Ivy saying that she'd love to have the historic school on the tour next year. She gushed about how people could not stop from raving about the old school building, the wood floors in the hallway and the gymnasium. Quite a few people sat at desks and spent time remembering their elementary school days. And Anne wasn't the only one keeping Ivy updated.

Josh texted multiple times during the afternoon, giving her reports on his visitors. She knew the train around his tree was a hit. Many people stopped in her shop afterward, asking her to look up the Lionel train cars in certain makes and models. She'd placed more than one order for train cars and the customers didn't even mind that the trains wouldn't be in by Christmas. Everyone was happy just to have a special train car to add to their holiday decorations in upcoming years. A few announced they were starting a new hobby collecting trains.

"Ivy!" Paige knocked on the shop door. She stood outside with her blue rain jacket pulled up around her head. She carried a blue basket of the slip-on booties the tour requested guests wear when they traipsed through homes.

Ivy twisted the knob and pulled the door open. She hadn't heard from Paige all afternoon.

"Did everything go okay at your house?"

"Oh my gosh," Paige said, her voice high and excited. "This was the most fun I've had in a long time. I'm going to open two more of the basic dog class in January, and I've got more requests for reading therapy dog teams than I know what to do."

The reading dog therapy teams. Ivy tried practicing with Max, but it was not going well. Despite multiple treats, Max would not sit down while she read aloud to him. And her reading wasn't getting better. The Holiday Express was in three days, and she had to do something, especially now that Josh helped her save the Holiday Homes Tour. She could not stumble her way through the simple holiday books as Mrs. Claus.

"Paige," Ivy said, her heart pounding. She had to ask Paige for help. She needed a reading therapy dog team to help her with her confidence. "I have to read holiday books to the children at the North Pole for the Holiday Express Train and…"

"That's a wonderful idea!" Paige said. "The children are going to love reading time with Mrs. Claus!"

"No." Ivy shook her head, the words struggled in her throat. She'd never admitted to anyone that she struggled with reading. But it was time. She had to do this. She had to do this for Josh to show him how much he meant to her this season. The cookie making, the tree decorating, all of it were things she had participated in joyfully, just like it was supposed to be and she had one person to thank for that joy—Josh.

"Reading aloud is hard for me," Ivy said. "I know the words, but my words trip up on my tongue. I moved around a lot in elementary school and just never caught up with my reading."

"Confidence!" Paige said. "You need confidence in reading aloud like the kids."

"Yes," Ivy said. "Do you think?" It was so hard for her to admit that she needed help, but she had to do it. "I don't want to let Josh down by fumbling my role of Mrs. Claus."

"You and Josh are so great together," Paige said, her eyes twinkled. "I can see why you don't want to disappoint him."

"Yes," Ivy said. "Josh has been my friend for a long time. He and my brother, Keith, and I." She flushed thinking of Josh and his lips on hers, the kiss in front of his Christmas tree. They were more than friends and she knew it. But she couldn't risk losing the friendship she'd treasured for so long by admitting her feelings were much stronger than friendship. His bright, sparkling eyes, the way he listened and knew just what to say, the way he protected everyone he knew.

"I don't know." Paige shook her head. "It seems to me

that he looks at you as more than a friend. Are you sure that's all there is between you two?"

Ivy's heart contracted. She liked Josh. A lot more than a friend. And maybe he did look at her the way Paige was saying, but she also didn't want to have her heart broken again. "It's not so simple."

"It never is," Paige said, and sighed. "I had my heart broken a few years ago. I haven't allowed myself to fall in love with anyone since. It's much easier to focus on my dog business."

"Yes," Ivy said. "I feel the same way about the antique shop." Something inside Ivy opened. Something that closed when her best friend, Katie, fell in love with Sawyer and moved it to the large sprawling barn on his property. Of course, she was happy for Katie, but she missed her. She missed the comradery of trying to build their businesses. She missed the light on next door, deep into the winter nights, the same way hers was as they worked through bookkeeping, online orders, and the day-to-day operations of a shop being run by one woman.

Katie taught her a lot about running the antique shop. She'd been there to listen when a customer complained. She'd listened when Ivy couldn't figure out how to set up the online shop and offered her own website wizard techs. She'd been there for Ivy, and she missed her. She'd built a wall around herself because she didn't want to risk becoming friends with Paige and having her leave t,oo. But it was time to take down that wall. She kept too many walls around herself, trying to protect herself from the heartache of losing the people she loved. But sometimes you had to risk that heartache and let people inside.

"But our businesses can't love us back," Paige said, her voice quiet. "Love doesn't come around all the time. It's important to step out and meet it when it arrives. Does Josh know how you feel about him?"

Ivy twirled a piece of ribbon through her fingers. "No," she whispered. "I haven't told him." Paige was right. Love didn't come along all the time. She needed to acknowledge her feelings for Josh. She needed to stop running away from them. She needed to open herself up to the possibility of telling Josh how she felt. It didn't mean her friendship with Josh would end, and maybe it meant that her friendship with Josh would move to a deeper level. A level she hadn't allowed herself to dream was possible.

"Take the risk," Paige said. "It's Christmas. There is magic at Christmas."

"You're right. But first," Ivy twirled her hands in the air. "Do you think I could read to one of your dog teams?" Ivy wasn't quite sure how the reading dog therapy teams worked. But it had to be better than trying to cajole Max to sit beside her while she read.

"Of course!" Paige said, but she frowned. "But we only have a few days before the Holiday Express, and I don't have any reading dog teams available right now."

Ivy's heart fell. "I understand. It's the holidays and everyone is busy."

"My certification with Willow lapsed and I don't go to

the schools and libraries. But Willow can sit with you while you practice reading." Paige pulled out her phone and scrolled through a roll of photos. "Here we are!" She held the phone out to Ivy.

Ivy exhaled and leaned over to look at the photo of Paige sitting beside a black cocker spaniel while a child read aloud to the dog. "I really appreciate this offer."

"Why don't we start now?" Paige asked. "We can go next door. Willow is ten but he will sit for an hour at a time with a few treats." She smiled. "If we pick out two or three books for you to read, we can do a couple a day over the next few days."

"I will get the book basket from Katie," Ivy said. "I'll select a few books, practice, and then place those on top and choose those to read on Christmas Eve."

"It's a deal!" Paige started toward the front door. "I'll run home and get Willow and take him out before he sits with you to get the wiggles out."

"Wait," Ivy lifted the key to the door from the small hook in her office. "There's another door."

Paige turned and frowned. "Another door?"

Ivy walked to the back left side of her shop and slipped the key into the door lock. She turned the knob and opened the door to Paige's dog training classroom.

"I wondered if that opened!" Paige said. "But I didn't see any locks from my side. I kept meaning to ask Bryan about it. He didn't mentioned it when he showed me the place to rent."

"It only opens from this side," Ivy said. "Katie and I used to keep it open all the time. We loved popping in to ask each other questions or have a quick snack together."

"I know you miss having her next door," Paige touched Ivy's arm.

"Yes," Ivy nodded. "I do." It was the first time Ivy acknowledged how much she missed Katie. She was happy for Katie and her new area in the barn, but she missed her. She missed having her slip in for a quick cup of coffee or to commiserate when another order fell through. She missed having that best friend next door to share those moments both of them needed to share before they returned home for the night.

"I can't take her place," Paige said. "But I'd like to be friends, Ivy."

Ivy nodded. It was time. It was time to accept Paige was next door. Paige was a hard worker. She jumped into Cranberry Bay Business Association, and she did have good ideas. It was time to include her as a part of the women she called friends in Cranberry Bay.

"Would you like to come to the gift-wrapping party tomorrow?" Ivy asked.

"Gift wrapping party?"

"It's a special event for the Holiday Express," Ivy said. "A small group of us meet at Bryan's real estate office. We spread the presents out, check the lists from the children and then wrap and label the gifts."

"I would love that!" Paige said. "I love to gift wrap! My pet customers don't always appreciate my skills." She grinned.

"It will be fun to have you on board." Ivy opened the

door between their shops and motioned for Paige to go first. "I'll leave my side unlocked and you can come over anytime you want."

"I'm so glad we're going to be friends," Paige said, hugging Ivy.

Chapter 16

Josh opened the legs of the folding table. On the other end, Adam hoisted the table upright. Adam reached into his flannel shirt pocket and unfolded a piece of paper. "I've got the list of all the children's names and the gifts they requested."

"Sawyer!" Katie placed her hands on her hips. She wore black leggings and a white sweatshirt with a hood. Her hair was pulled into a ponytail on top of her head. Small wisps dangled around her face. "The gifts should go on this end of the table." She frowned at him.

"Just taking a rest," he winked at her. Sawyer wore a deep, navy blue sweatshirt with dark jeans and work boots. A ballcap with Portland Timbers tilted at an angle, and he reached up to straighten it.

Josh resisted the urge to laugh. Katie and Sawyer struggled to let go of who was in charge.

"These are fantastic!" Bryan turned over a box of Legos to build a small ship. "Haven't seen this set since I was a child." He knelt in front of a large stack of toys. He wore his usual outfit of dark jeans and a sweatshirt. Bryan only got into dress clothes when he was showing a prospective business partner from Seattle or Portland a piece of property, which in Cranberry Bay was not very often. Cranberry Bay didn't draw investors to the small Craftsman homes dotting the hillside above the river. Those investors went to the beach towns, looking for summer vacation rentals and hotel ownership opportunities.

"And they are for a child," Rylee leaned down and swept the box away from him. She kissed the top of his head. Rylee looked as comfortable as Katie with her grey leggings and light blue zip up sweatshirt. She wore her hair pulled back in a scrunchy, away from her face.

"And look at this truck!" Bryan picked up a toy truck and spun the wheels.

"Boys!" Rylee shook her head, her grin wide and her eyes focused only on Bryan. The two bonded together by the love they shared.

The countdown to the Holiday Express had begun. The twenty-four-hour mark was here. Tonight, they'd wrap the gifts. Tomorrow night, the train would head for the North Pole with the children aboard. His stomach churned with sadness at taking the first holiday train express run without his grandfather. And at the same time, there was a bubbling of excitement at playing the Santa role with Ivy as Mrs. Claus. And there was the worry of how the new location and route would be perceived by the town.

Sasha placed a tray of cookies beside a large silver urn filled with coffee. "Treats are here!" She wiped her hands on a festive holiday apron covering her short black skirt, leggings, and red tennis shoes. Like Josh, Sasha lived and breathed Christmas. She wore a festive elf hat with bells, and a holiday sweater with a large Mr. Grinch.

"Save me a gingerbread man," Bryan said, from his spot on the floor by the toys.

"Did you bring the chocolate crinkles?" Adam set the list down on the table and strode toward Sasha.

"Hello!" Ivy pulled open the door to the large room. She wore a festive red and white holiday sweater, jeans, and her hair was pulled back with a green headband with elf ears attached.

Josh jiggled his feet. He wanted to break into song. Ivy had gotten into the Christmas spirit.

Paige walked in front of her and carried a large plastic tub filled with wrapping paper. Rolls stuck out at all ends, and Paige peered around them. "Where should I set the wrapping paper?" Cranberry Bay didn't own that many places for gathering. The small City Hall chamber room, the library, and a large room at the back of the pub. Sometimes Bryan shared empty buildings that were for rent. He'd open them up for the night and local groups could use them for meetings with a set of tables and chairs Bryan kept in a storage unit.

"Paige?" Sasha turned to Ivy and raised an eyebrow.

Josh smothered his grin. Ivy mended her rift with Paige and invited Paige to the gift wrapping.

"Paige is going to help us," Ivy said, her voice clear

and strong. "She's been a great addition to the Cranberry Bay Business Association, and it'd be nice to have her involved with the Holiday Express."

"Good to see you, Paige!" Katie waved at her. "Set the gift wrap in the middle of the table. We get a little wrapping train going and pass the presents along."

Sasha picked up a small white cookie and strode down the linoleum floor of the hall. She stopped in front of the bows. "I will do the bows."

"I'll sort the toys!" Bryan picked up the list with the children's names and items requested.

"You'll never give them to us to wrap." Rylee nudged him with her side. "You can't spend all night looking through each one and wanting it for yourself."

"I wouldn't do that," Bryan turned to her and placed a kiss on her nose.

Katie stepped to the name cards. "I'll attach the cards to each package. Sawyer will help me."

"So bossy," Sawyer said and grinned at Katie.

Katie flushed but smiled at him. The look in her eyes as she gazed at Sawyer said it all. The two of them were well matched and respected each other for the strength they each had, but at the same time, there was a softness around them. A private circle they created with their love for each other.

"I'll help with the wrapping paper," Gracie said.

"I can help too," Adam said, and stepped up beside Gracie. His face flushed.

Josh studied his friend. Adam kept to himself, working on the park trails. He was quiet and thoughtful.

But so was Gracie. She kept to herself, her music and running her inn. Was Adam developing feelings for Gracie?

"Ivy, can you help load the toys into the bags," Katie asked, and pointed to the large burlap sacks which would get loaded onto the back of the train. The elves would go through each bag, flipping over the tags to see what was inside the item before handing them out at the North Pole.

"Yes," Rylee nodded. "As Mrs. Claus, you'll have to help Santa hand out the toys."

"Did someone say Santa?" Josh asked. He stepped toward Ivy.

"Ivy needs help," Rylee called. "She's loading the wrapped toys into the bag." She pulled a sheet of red paper with small Santa's across the page and cut it in a straight line. Carefully, she laid the large toy truck across the page and folded the edges to meet the edges of the box.

Josh leaned closer to Ivy. "Where is your list?"

"I didn't bring my list," Ivy said, and smiled at Josh.

"No list?" Josh leaned closer to her. His heart filled with joy at her smile.

Sasha turned on the music and the sound of holiday carols filled the room. She moved her hips in time to jazzy jingle bells as she wrapped a bow across a long, flat package.

"Remember this one?" Josh asked. How could she forget this version of *Rocking Around the Christmas Tree?* The song they listened to at every holiday work party, starting with when they were in high school. They even made up their own dance to the tune.

Ivy grinned.

"Want to dance?" Josh held out his hand.

Ivy stared at it for a minute and then looked into his eyes. He felt himself melting in them.

She took his hand and in one swoop, he sailed her across the linoleum floor and moved her into the steps they created together. Swirls and twirls. She looked into his eyes and smiled.

His heart turned over. He couldn't deny his feelings. He liked Ivy as far more than a friend, he always had. It started with the kiss so long ago. And it was time to tell her. It was time to stop pretending. It was time to take the risk and find the happiness that his friends experienced when they'd finally surrendered to the women they loved.

Sasha let out loud cat calls as Josh sashed closer to Ivy. He pulled her into his arms, not caring that the music hadn't slowed. Her heart pounded with his, and she pressed against him. He shifted his hands down her lower back.

As the music finished, Ivy looked up at him, her cheeks flushed and her eyes bright. He leaned close to her. His lips pressed against her ear. "Thanks for the dance, Ivy."

Clapping filled the room and Josh linked his hand with Ivy's. They turned toward his friends, clustered in a group around the wrapped presents.

"I didn't know you could dance like that, brother." Suzanne stood at the doorway and beside her, Kami. She wore a black leather coat pulled over black slacks, small black heeled pumps, and a paisley top. Kami looked like she was ready for a dinner out in Seattle. Pink gloss covered her lips, her brows were etched and sculpted, and a perfectly blended mix of browns and tans blended on her eyeshadow.

"Are we interrupting?" Kami asked. Her eyes searched Josh's face.

Chapter 17

Ivy slipped her hand out of Josh's and took a step back. The music continued to play but the voices of her friends were silent. The clapping stopped. From the road, a large semi-truck barreled past and the noise crashed into Ivy's emotions.

"You didn't interrupt," Josh stood rooted in place. "We're glad to see you. Welcome back to Cranberry Bay."

Ivy walked to the wrapping table. She picked up a set of colored pencils and unrolled a piece of wrapping paper. She lay it on the tab beside the colored pencils. *Breathe. They got swept up in the moment. Nothing more. Breathe.* But her breath felt shallow and uneven. She couldn't keep pretending that her feelings for Josh were nothing more than friendship.

The voices of her friends resumed around her, only a bit less festive. The music swirled at her from the small speaker in the corner of the room.

"Ivy?" Sasha placed her hand on Ivy's arm. "Are you okay?"

"Mmmm." Ivy folded the paper around the colored pencils. She creased the sides and made sure it covered the entire box.

"You don't have to pretend," Sasha said, her voice lowered.

"I think I'll get some tea." Ivy pushed the wrapped present aside. "My stomach feels a little upset." Josh moved from the middle of the room and stood talking with Kami in the far-left corner. Suzanne stood next to Katie, who handed her a packet of gift cards with pens. She pointed to the list of children's names and requested presents.

Ivy turned away from them and walked toward the small pot filled with water. Her hands shook as she poured. She'd dropped her guard. She'd allowed her feelings for Josh to move her to feel again, feel the magic of Christmas again. And now all of that felt too exposed. Too raw. Too vulnerable.

"Here is some breakfast tea." Sasha unwrapped a tea bag and plunged it into the water. "I don't see anything else."

"Thanks," Ivy said. She felt wooden, stiff. She knew she needed to get back to wrapping the gifts for the Holiday Express, but she didn't know if her legs would carry her across the room.

"Why don't we go to the bakery for a few minutes?" Sasha said. "I have chamomile tea, your favorite."

Ivy nodded. "That sounds nice." She would take a

few minutes and center herself. Then return and finish wrapping presents. She could get her emotions back in place, where they belonged.

"Hey, everyone!" Sasha waved her arms. "Ivy and I need to run over to the bakery. Stock up on the cookies. We'll be right back."

Ivy didn't look at Josh. She pulled on her coat, grabbed her purse, and hurried behind Sasha and into the cool, winter air. The blast of rain hit her face and her tears mixed with the rainwater.

"Come on." Sasha tossed her arm around her. "It'll be warm in the bakery."

Ivy allowed herself to be led across the street and into the bakery. Sasha turned on the lights and walked over to the small gas stove. She flicked the switch and the gas logs blazed to life. Ivy pulled out one of the small chairs beside a glass table next to the gas fireplace and sat down.

"It's my fault," Ivy said. "I let myself get carried away, carried away with Christmas fantasies. I believed in happily ever after when I know happily ever after with Josh isn't possible."

Sasha poured hot water into two mugs and, carrying a basket of teas over to Ivy, she sat down opposite her.

"Josh cares about you," Sasha said. "There is a spark when he looks at you, the way he danced with you."

"Yes," Ivy said, "Josh has always cared about me. But we are friends. Kami is who Josh loves."

"I don't know," Sasha shook her head. "I'm not sure."

"What do you mean?" Ivy looked up at her friend.

"I've heard things this fall," Sasha said. "You know

how I try not to pay attention to people's talk around here, but it's hard sometimes. She took that job in Seattle and...."

"It doesn't matter." Ivy took a sip of the tea, the hot liquid settling her stomach. "I just let myself get too carried away." Ivy tightened her lips. But was that the truth? Had she let herself get too carried away or was she just realizing that her feelings for Josh were much stronger than she believed possible? That maybe it wasn't possible to just be friends with him? That maybe she did want something more and she might be willing to risk the friendship she'd treasured for years.

"No, you didn't," Sasha leaned forward, her hands holding onto Ivy's arms. "You didn't get too carried away. You followed your heart. For the first time since I've known you, you didn't try to hide in your lists or your schedule. You need to tell him how you feel."

Ivy shook her head. "I don't know if I can."

"Yes," Sasha said. "You need to do this. Don't miss the moment. It's not about Kami. It's about you. You've carried this for so long. We've all known how you felt."

Ivy turned away from Sasha. "I thought I kept my feelings hidden."

Sasha shook her head. "We are your friends, and we always knew. Now, he needs to know. He needs to know that you love him."

"I don't know." Ivy dunked her tea bag into the water. She loved Josh. She loved how he encouraged her to look at the bright side. She loved how he showed her the spirit of Christmas. She loved how he held her, as if nothing else mattered in the world. But did she have the courage to tell him that?

Sasha took a long drink of her tea. "It's something I wish I had another chance to do."

Ivy studied her friend. Sasha didn't talk about her college boyfriend, Greg. Ivy knew Sasha met Greg in college, became pregnant with Tyler, and moved to Cranberry Bay to run her aunt's bakery. Greg hadn't been a part of Tyler's life, and Ivy wasn't sure if that was Greg's choice or Sasha's choice or both.

"We need to tell people in our lives that we love them," Sasha said. "Don't let it pass you by."

Ivy mulled Sasha's words over. Did she have the courage to tell Josh how she felt? Did she have the courage to risk the friendship she loved for the possibility of something more?

Chapter 18

"**K**ami." Josh crossed his arms and leaned back. He studied Kami. "What are you doing here?"

"I wanted to surprise you!" Kami said, her voice bright and cheerful. "Holiday surprise!"

"You did surprise me," he said. Kami was a beautiful woman, and she'd make someone very happy, but that man wasn't him. He wasn't in love with her, and she deserved to be with someone who was in love with her.

"I just got into town. Suzanne told me about the gift wrapping, and we thought it'd be fun to surprise everyone. Don't you think so?" Kami leaned close to him.

Josh's chest constricted. Kami was his longtime girl-friend, but they grew apart. The end was inevitable. What they wanted had changed. He wanted to live in Cranberry Bay and raise a family. She wanted to be in the city, travel, and explore the world. And he wasn't in love with her. He didn't know if he had ever really been in love with her. Kami was who he was expected to be with. But he didn't want to do what he was expected to do. He wanted to follow his heart. And his heart was with Ivy.

All around Josh, the voices of his friends buzzed with excitement as they wrapped presents and worked to get the Holiday Express ready. He needed to help them. He was in charge of this event now that his grandfather was gone. "I really need to get back to helping." Josh waved his arm over the bustling room.

"I hear you are driving the train and playing Santa," Kami said. "Who is playing Mrs. Claus?" She pressed closer to him and touched his arm.

"Ivy." Josh's heart quickened as her name rolled over his lips.

"Ivy?" Kami took a step backward and removed her arm.

"You and I want different things," Josh said and exhaled. "It's time to admit that. You deserve to be with a man who can give you what you want. But that man is not me."

"That's why you never called me back." Kami stepped away from him. Her voice was cold.

"Because I didn't know what to say. But I do now. I'll always care about you, Kami. But that's not enough. You deserve someone who loves you. Really loves you."

"Yes," Kami clutched her leather bag closer to her. "I guess I've known we were over. I should go. I don't know what I was thinking…"

"Stay," Josh said. "We'd love to have you help us.

You're a long-time resident of Cranberry Bay, and this is a holiday tradition."

Suzanne danced up to them. "You're going to come for the holiday brunch at our house on Christmas Day, right?" She looped her hand through Kami's arm. "It will be just like old times."

Josh held his breath. He'd invited Ivy to the holiday brunch. He wasn't sure if she'd attend now. But he wanted her to be there. He wanted to celebrate Christmas morning with her.

"No," Kami shook her head and looked at Josh. "I can't make it this year. I'm sorry, Suz. But we'll get together and go have a meal sometime while I'm home."

Josh exhaled. "Thank you,"

Kami nodded and turned away and headed for the door.

"What happened?" Suzanne stared after Kami. "I thought the two of you were going to get engaged."

Josh exhaled. It was time to start telling the truth to his friends and family.

"Kami and I want different things," Josh said. "We've been on a break since she moved to Seattle."

"She didn't say anything to me." Suzanne placed her hands on her hips. Her lips formed a tight line.

"We weren't ready to tell people," Josh said. "We weren't ready to face the disappointment of letting people down."

Suzanne exhaled. "I know what you mean."

Josh peered at his sister. He saw the dark circles under her eyes concealed behind a thick layer of make-up. Ivy was right. Everything was not okay with Suzanne. He lowered his voice. "What's wrong, Suz?"

"Everything." Suzanne's eyes welled with tears. "I was trying so hard to pretend and keep it all together. But I was fired from my coaching job. I haven't been able to deliver the results the University wants in the team."

Josh placed his arm around his sister's shoulders. "I'm sorry. I know how much swimming has always meant to you." And he did know. Suzanne's entire life revolved around swimming.

"I think I wanted to be fired," Suzanne said, her voice choked with tears. "My heart just wasn't in swimming anymore. I met someone and…"

"You met someone?" Josh peered at Suzanne. He'd never known Suzanne to fall in love with anyone. She was in love with swimming.

"It didn't work out," Suzanne said. "I spent too much time with swimming. I gave my whole life to swimming. And I missed so much." She waved her hand over the crowded room. "I missed all of this, the friendship, the laughter, the love, the joy of the season."

"It's not too late," Josh said.

"I know," Suzanne said. "That's why I'm not going back to Seattle. I'm going to stay in Cranberry Bay. I've already talked to Gavin at the high school. He said I can teach PE. It'll be a start until I figure out what I want to do."

"That's great!" Josh pulled his sister in for a big hug. "I'm happy you're staying in Cranberry Bay."

"Me too," Suzanne pulled away from him. "And

maybe next year I can have a part on the Holiday Express."

"Of course, you can!" Josh said. "We will make sure you have a big role to play on the train!"

"Josh!" Adam whistled at him from across the room. "Need your hands!"

"We'll talk later," Suzanne said. "I'm going to go find Kami. I think we need to talk, too."

"Great idea." Josh gave Suzanne another hug and then crossed the room and stepped up beside Adam. He reached over and turned the holiday music down. "What needs to be done?"

Adam looked at him. "You okay?"

"Yes," Josh exhaled. And he was okay. For the first time, the feelings inside him weren't conflicted. He'd connected with Suzanne in a way he hadn't done since they were children. And he'd been honest with Kami. The relief flooded him. He didn't have to fight his feelings for Ivy. Now, all he needed to do was tell her the truth he kept bottled up inside him for years.

Chapter 19

I vy slipped into the red dress. The train rocked as it rolled toward the North Pole. She held onto the small sink to steady herself and stared at the mirror. Her eyes looked unusually bright with all the emotion swirling inside. The Mrs. Claus dress came out beautifully with a scoop neck, fitted tightly around her and swirled into a skirt. Ivy grabbed the gingham apron. It tied around her waist, and she wished it would tie around her body and take away that little something extra.

From outside the car, the excited children's voices mounted as the train rumbled closer to the North Pole. Ivy tucked the small Santa hat earrings into each pierced earring hole. They sparkled in the light as she turned her head.

The train boarding ran smoothly, each child presenting the golden Holiday Express ticket and was shepherded into the waiting train cars. Most of the children wore the lazy pants pajamas under their coats. Their parents had picked them up earlier that afternoon before the train ride. The steam from the black engine drifted around the train in a smokey haze as the parents stood on the boarding platform and waved to the children nestled into the cars and peering out the windows.

It'd been easy to avoid thinking about her feelings toward Josh in the boarding process. But now, as the train rocked and rolled toward the North Pole, Ivy's stomach clenched with emotion.

A knock on the door startled Ivy out of her thoughts, and she pulled it open.

"Ready?" Paige asked. She wore one of the traditional Holiday Express Elf outfits, a green pantsuit and a green hat with elf ears.

"I think so," Ivy exhaled. She wasn't ready. She would never be ready for this moment of playing Mrs. Claus alongside Josh, but it was time, and she wouldn't let the children down.

"You can do this," Paige said. "We've practiced, and you know the stories. Just remember to breathe."

Ivy exhaled. "I can do this." Her heart pounded. She could do it. She worked for the last three days with Paige and Willow, practicing reading aloud. They'd found an easy *Night Before Christmas*, and she read the story aloud to Paige's dog, making sure she knew each word and did not stumble or stutter.

Ivy followed Paige into the train car and stood at the small doorway. When the train stopped, she'd get off and slip in through the back side of Santa's Workshop. Ivy's heart crashed against her throat. She'd read the story to the children while Josh changed into his Santa suit, and then he'd join her beside the makeshift fireplace. Together, they'd handout the gifts to the children.

The train slowed amid a twinkle of lights and a small makeshift boarding platform with a wood sign, "North Pole." Sasha's vintage trailer glowed with red and green twinkling lights and a blazing bonfire burned to the far left of Katie's transformed barn. A white Santa's Workshop sign glowed with red and white lights.

"Welcome to the North Pole!" Katie called from her spot on the platform. "Santa will be arriving soon."

The train rolled to a stop, and Ivy hopped down onto the platform beside Katie.

"Your hat is in the back room," Katie said and smiled at her. "I just finished a few last stitches."

Ivy took a deep breath and hurried down the pathway and into the barn. The room transformed into a lighted, glowing Santa's workshop. She hurried to the back room and stopped to pick up the small white knit hat. She placed it on her head and, with a few bobby pins, adjusted the hat so it wouldn't fall off. Her hair framed her face in small curls.

Ivy stepped back into the room and froze. "Santa."

Josh stood beside the make-believe fireplace.

He turned and gazed at her. "Ivy." Josh cleared his throat. "Mrs. Claus, I mean."

Josh wasn't supposed to be here yet. She was supposed to read to the children and allow him time to get into his costume. But he was in his costume. And he would be here while she read.

Ivy nodded and stepped to the plush red chair by the makeshift fireplace. She reached into the basket and pulled out the Night Before Christmas. She held it on her lap and tried to steady her hands.

"Ivy," Josh said. "I…"

"And here is Santa's workshop!" Katie's voice called as children's voices filled the air.

Ivy smiled as she turned toward the door, and the children piled into the room. Her insides shook but she tried to remain calm. She motioned the children toward the red carpet in front of the two chairs, and they walked forward with wide eyes.

"Santa!" cried a young girl wearing red and green pajama pants and her hair bound into pigtails.

"Ho. Ho. Ho," Josh boomed. "Merry Christmas!"

Katie, Rylee, and Gracie worked to get the children situated on the rug so each could see Ivy and Santa.

"Mrs. Claus has a story for you," Katie placed her hands to her lips. "Shhh."

Ivy picked up the book from her lap. She raised it to eye level for the children and opened the first page. The words blurred. She blinked. Her heart pounded. She could do this. She'd practiced. She knew the words. She knew the pacing. She knew the tone of how to read the story.

But she couldn't open her mouth.

The room around her stilled.

"Mrs. Claus?" Josh leaned forward.

Ivy looked up and into his eyes, his sparkling eyes that she'd known since she first arrived in Cranberry Bay. His eyes telling her, affirming that she could do it. She could read the story. Josh had always been sure of her. His presence was calm and solid. Holding her steady.

"Once upon a time," Ivy opened her mouth and the words she'd practiced flowed out.

When she finished, Josh reached into the first bag behind him. He pulled out one of the wrapped presents with the name on it and read it aloud. A little girl stepped forward and shyly took the teddy bear he held out.

Ivy leaned around her chair and pulled out the bag placed beside it. She opened the tie handles and handed Josh another present. The two worked steadily, handing out each gift to every child. Sounds of glee and excitement filled the air as the children unwrapped the presents.

"And there is one final present." Josh reached into the velvet bag.

Ivy frowned. How could there be one more present?

Josh pulled a small red box out of the bag. "This one is for Mrs. Claus."

Ivy took the present. Her fingers touched Josh's fingers. "For me?" This wasn't part of the scripted Holiday Express event.

"Hot cocoa is ready!" Sasha stood with a tray of hot cocoa in the open doorway of Santa's Workshop.

The children jumped up and scattered across the room.

The unopened present lay in Ivy's lap.

Chapter 20

"Hot cocoa!" Josh stood and patted his belly. The children laughed and a few rushed forward to hug him and then dashed toward the tables with hot cocoa.

When the children settled at the tables, Josh turned to Ivy. "Open the present, Ivy," he said, his voice soft.

Ivy turned the box over and opened the wrap. She lifted the lid and gasped. She pulled out a green wreath pin. She turned it over and tears welled in her eyes. "It's just like my mom's pin."

Josh nodded. "I called Keith. He told me about it. I got on the internet and scoured some thrift shops. This one popped up in Arizona. I don't think it's your pin, but it's close…"

Ivy's hands shook. Josh stepped forward and lifted the pin from the box. He pinned it to the top of Ivy's dress, inhaling her scent and feeling her softness underneath his fingers. When he finished, he didn't move away from her.

"I need to tell you something," Ivy said, her voice trembling.

"No," Josh said. "I want to tell you something first." He took a deep breath and exhaled. "I'm in love with you, Ivy. I have been for a very long time. I convinced myself that friendship was safer. I hid behind my relationship with Kami. But I couldn't fight my feelings anymore."

Ivy stepped closer to him. She looked up into his eyes. "I love you, Josh. That's what I wanted to tell you. I have loved you since that first kiss on the Holiday Express."

Josh leaned toward her as Sawyer's voice boomed. "Time to board the train!"

"Come on," Josh held out his hand to Ivy.

She slipped her hand in his, and he led her to the front of the train.

Katie, Gracie, and Sawyer hustled the children through the hot cocoa line and rounded them up.

Josh motioned Ivy to get into the front of the train using the small footstool. He hopped in behind her, smiled at her, and started the engine.

The steam engine hummed to life and Josh raised the whistle. A long, deep sound in the dark of the winter's night. The rain turned into small snowflakes and a flurry filled the sky.

"Merry Christmas, Ivy," Josh said as he put his arm around her and pulled her close. He lowered his lips to hers as the snow swirled around the train, the whistle blew, and he kissed the woman he loved.

"Merry Christmas," Ivy murmured against his lips.

Merry Christmas.

Holiday Cut-Out Cookies

<u>Josh and Ivy's Christmas Cut-Out Cookies</u>
  2/3 C shortening
  3/4 C sugar
  1/2 tsp grated orange peel or orange juice
  1/2 tsp vanilla
  1 egg
  4 teaspoons of milk
  2 C sifted flour
  1 ½ tsp baking powder
  1/4 tsp salt

Cream shortening, sugar, orange peel, and vanilla. Add egg, beat until light and fluffy. Stir in milk. Sift dry ingredients and blend with creamed mixture. Divide dough in half. Chill one hour.

Roll out and shape with cookie cutters. Bake on greased cookie sheets for about 6-8 minutes, but time will vary according to oven. Cool. Decorate with icing and sprinkles. Makes 2 dozen.

Powdered Sugar Icing
  1 C powdered sugar
  ¼ tsp vanilla
  Milk

Mix powdered sugar, vanilla, and one tablespoon of milk. Stir in milk one tablespoon at a time until of drizzled consistency.

Holiday Spritz Cookies

<u>Holiday Spritz Cookies</u>
  1 C powdered sugar
  1 C butter softened
  1/2 tsp almond flavoring
  1 egg
  2 1/3 C all-purpose flour
  1/4 tsp salt

Heat oven to 400 degrees. In a large bowl, beat powdered sugar, butter, vanilla, and egg until light and fluffy. Stir in flour and salt, blend well. Fit cookie press with desired plate. Fill cookie press, press dough onto ungreased cookie sheets. Bake at 400 degrees for 5 to 7 minutes or until lightly browned on edges Immediately remove from cookie sheets. Cool completely.

Acknowledgments

Thank you to the weekly support of the Rose City RWA Monday Night sprint group who kept me writing during the pandemic. I could not have written this story without your cheerleading and weekly goal setting to keep me on track. The story was inspired by the Oregon Coast Scenic Railroad which offers fun, informative, and scenic train rides along the Oregon Coast including a Holiday Train. The Holiday Express sponsored by the Oregon Rail Heritage Center in Portland, Oregon runs near my house at Christmas and provides many joyful weekends listening to the loud whistle, steam engine and the blinking holiday lights.

During my research, I visited the Portland Chapter of the Train Collector's Association Open House and Train Meet. Instantly, I was transported back to the days of childhood when my dad collected trains and the clickity-clack of the cars as they sped around the tracks. Dad set the trains up in the basement, on a large piece of wood held up by two sawhorses. My brother and I were warned repeatedly not to touch the trains. However, my brother could never resist running the controls when Dad wasn't around. A few pieces often disappeared or broke after those forbidden runs!

And finally thank you to my readers of the Cranberry Bay series who have waited a long time for the third book in the series. And for all of those who have asked, "When are you going to write a holiday romance?" It's here!

About the Author

Mindy Hardwick holds an MFA in Writing for Children and Young Adults from Vermont College. Her published contemporary romance includes her Cranberry Bay Series: *Sweetheart Cottage* and *Sweetheart Summer*. She has also published a young adult romance, *Weaving Magic* and a young adult novella, *Erin's Choice*.

Mindy's middle grade books include: *The World is a Sniff, Stained Glass Summer, Some Stories Are Not Seen, and Seymour's Secret*. Mindy facilitated a poetry workshop for teens at Denney Juvenile Justice Center and wrote about the experience in her memoir, *Kids in Orange: Voices from Juvenile Detention*.

Mindy can often be found walking with her cocker spaniel on the north Oregon Coast beaches. Visit her website: www. mindyhardwick.com to find out about new releases, upcoming events or to book her to speak to your class or school group.

Sign up for her newsletter here.

Also by Mindy Hardwick

Middle Grade

Stained Glass Summer

Some Stories Are Not Seen

The World Is a Sniff

Seymour's Secret

Young Adult

Weaving Magic

Kids In Orange: Voices from Juvenile Detention

Erin's Choice

Sweet Contemporary Romance

Sweetheart Cottage

Sweetheart Summer

Sweetheart Christmas

The World Is a Sniff

My Name

The first thing everyone asks my Human is, "What type of dog is he?"

My Human explains I am a Cocker Spaniel. Sometimes I have shaggy fur, which hangs in my eyes, and sometimes I have short fur my Human calls a seal coat. I once wore the Cocker skirt, which is long fur along the sides and a short cut on top, but after a bad groom where the groomer cut off some of the fur skirt but not all of it, that was the end of my Cocker skirt. Bad grooms are something I have a lot of, but that's a story for another day.

The second question quickly follows the first. "Is he purebred?"

I guess everyone thinks because I am both black and tan and on the big size of an American Cocker Spaniel, I must not be purebred.

I am very purebred.

I come from a long linage of winning agility dogs and

my father was a show dog. My mom is a black Cocker with a white chest. I have the same markings as her on my chest. My uncle is a chocolate Cocker, which explains where I get my tan paws and bushy tan eyebrows. I have six brothers and sisters in my litter and it was the biggest litter my mom ever had. The litter before me only had one pup. That pup stayed at the Breeder Human's home with my mom, grandma, and uncle. She thinks she is a very special pup because there was only one of her and she is a year older than all of us.

But we know that our litter is the most special. We were born for magnificence.

Every day we eat specially cooked food. The Breeder Human holds each of us for a long time so we know we are loved. She places us in a laundry basket and potty trains us outside. People come to visit us all the time. The Humans take lots of pictures of us. They lift us and move our legs back and forth.

In the afternoons, we roll and tumble in a large pen filled with blankets and soft toys. The pen sits outside on a deck, and we get used to outside noises and smells. Our uncle, mother, and grandmother practice weaving between wobbling poles, balancing on teetering seesaws, and racing through canvas tunnels. We peer through the wire crates and dream of our days ahead filled with magnificence.

I am the first dog to climb out of the sleeping box. I waddle down the long hall and stare at the pictures of my uncle, mama, and grandma. There are also pictures of other dogs I don't know. All of the pictures have a lot of blue ribbons attached to the frames. This is what magnificence looks like. Sometimes the other dogs get into a big van and leave for a few days with the Humans. When they return, there are more ribbons on the wall. The dogs get fed special meals that smell delicious and my tummy growls with anticipation for when I will get those special meals.

One day, we are given a test. This is the beginning of magnificence. But it's been a bad morning for me. I got up on the wrong side of the pen. I snarled a couple of times at the other pups who got too close to my space. I hid the ball behind the Tester Human and peed on the floor. Magnificence slips out of my paws.

After the test, we are loaded back into a crate. We tumble over each other. The Humans talk about us. They look at the videos and they decide our fate. I separate myself from my littermates and press my nose against the crate and listen.

"The black and tan pup. He's a little aggressive. He might not be so suited to the agility life. He should be a pet dog."

"Pet dog?" I ask my littermates. I am going to be a pet dog? My heart quivers and I shake. I shake and shake and shake. What is a pet dog? How can I be a pet dog and still be magnificent?

I ask all the dogs in my family. But no one understands the job of a pet dog. Everyone has always been an agility dog. I tuck my stubby tail between my legs and curl into the corner of the pen. The other dogs roll and tumble and play. But I don't want to play. I am scared. I will not have ribbons by my picture in a hallway. I will not see my other littermates or family dogs at agility events. I will be off on my own as a pet dog. It is a fate worse than death. I can't stop shaking.

For the next couple of days, I pee outside. I eat as much as I can to fill my belly and follow all the Breeder Human's rules. The Breeder Human gives all of us our first puppy haircut. Everyone says I look the finest of all the dogs. My black and tan markings are striking. Maybe now someone will see how magnificent I am!

The next morning, two of my littermates are taken away and reappear in the yard next door. We all sniff each other through the fence. In their new yard, there are lots of poles and tunnels to teach them how to be magnificent!

That afternoon, someone arrives for my sister. The Human picks her up and holds her close. She coos at her and tells her she will be a magnificent agility dog. I sit very still. One by one my littermates leave for their magnificent lives. No one comes for me.

Maybe a pet dog means no one wanted me at all! I whimper.

But before I can go into a howl, a Human walks toward the pen. Her eyes glow and she smiles. I sniff. She smells like food and comfort and love. Lots of love.

My Human picks me up and holds me close to her chest. I remember her smell from when the Humans came to visit us. The day she visited, she liked my sister, but I knew my sister was already spoken for. That day, I snuggled deep into the Human's palm and tried to tell her I loved her. It must have worked because here she is —lifting me out and hugging me close!

My Human talks to my Breeder Human and takes a bag full of goodies for me. She carries me outside and places me in the back seat of a car. I have never been in a car before and it smells like adventure and excitement. There is a mid-sized Human in the back seat. My Human explains this is someone she is mentoring. I don't know what mentoring means, but I think it sounds like something nice. My Human must be a nice person to have this extra Human with her.

Suddenly, the car moves and speeds up. Everything spins around me. My stomach lurches and my breakfast lands all over the seat.

I shake and shake. I am sure I will never stop shaking. Someone let me out of this car. Whimpers and howls come out of me and I barely know it's me.

The Human stops the car and turns to look at me. "It's okay. First car rides make all dogs throw up."

I lay my head on the seat and close my eyes.

The small Human rubs my fur. I am really glad she is riding with me. Everything swirls and dances around me. I stop whimpering and howling but I can't stop shaking. I hope the car ride is over soon and I don't have to take very many of these in my new life.

It seems to take a long time, but eventually, the car stops. My Human lifts me out of the back seat. She carries me to a front porch and opens a door. An animal with a long tail and ears steps outside. Her tail swishes as she arches her back. She rubs against my Human.

Who is this strange fascinating animal? I try to sniff her. But she moves away, and I can't get close.

"This is Cleo, the cat," my Human says. "She lives here too."

The cat has the same colors as mine—black, tan, and white—but they look different on her. Tan, black and white fur swirls all over her body. The Human calls her calico. Cleo smells fun but she is very standoffish. Every time I try to get close to her to sniff her, she dances away like it's a game. I lean down on my front paws and growl and bark at her. I want to be best buddies and hope we sleep on top of each other in the same pen.

"Has the Human given you a name?" Cleo purrs.

"No." I paw the ground. I don't want to tell Cleo I have a name. The Breeder Human gave me a name. She said I had a little bit of an attitude. It wasn't my fault I snapped sometimes at the other pups in my litter. I just liked my space and they got too close and I had to tell them.

"Do you know what a pet dog is?" I ask Cleo.

Cleo winds among the porch posts. She still won't come near me. "No," she purrs. "But it doesn't sound good. I am not a pet cat. I am a cat."

I sit down and lay my head between my paws. I'm supposed to be magnificent but how can I be magnificent as a pet dog? I don't even know what a pet dog is supposed to do!

Cleo hops off the porch and rolls around in the grass. I want to join her and lunge toward her, but my Human captures me before I can leap off the porch.

"Stormy!" My Human says in a bright and cheery voice.

Stormy? I cock my head. What is a stormy?

The Human pets me. "I had another Cocker Spaniel. On the day she died, there was a big storm. On the way home from the veterinarian a rainbow came out. Your name will be the link between my two dogs."

The Human's voice is sad. I know what happens at those final veterinarian appointments. All dogs know those final vet appointments are where we say our forever goodbyes to our Humans. I lean against my Human. I don't want to say goodbye to her for a long, long time.

"Stormy." She rubs behind my ears. I press against her fingers.

Stormy.

I have a name.

Cleo's Sandbox Treats

The first night in my new home, my Human places me in a wire crate. It's much smaller than the one I've slept in with my littermates. But there is a soft cushion I don't have to share with my brothers and sisters who always took up too much space. My Human sits on the couch with a book and I try to keep an eye on her, but I'm very sleepy. It's been a big day and my eyes close. My Human's smell drifts around me and I feel safe.

A few hours later, the cat swishes by and flicks her tail against my crate. My eyes fly open. There are no warm littermates for me to snuggle against, it is very dark, and I can't smell my Human. I whimper as the fear overtakes me. I howl and cry.

My Human rushes into the room and flips on a switch. The room floods with light. She is holding a big pillow cushion and some blankets. It looks so warm and comfortable.

"Stormy?" She peers into my crate.

I smell her and stop crying, but I still whimper. I want out of here. I want to snuggle against her. I want to press myself against her so I know she is there. She doesn't understand how big this loneliness is in me. I've never felt something this horrible. I want out of the crate. I stand up on my hind legs and paw at the cage. "Please," I cry. "Please let me out."

"I knew this might happen tonight." My Human spreads out her pillow and blanket on the floor next to me.

I lie down with my nose at the crate door and stick my paw through the bars. I want her to take me out. I can sleep beside her on the big cushion pillow. I give her my best pleading look and whimper just a bit. "Take me out, please."

But my Human doesn't understand me. She sticks her hand into my crate and rubs my fur. It's better than nothing and after a long time, I close my eyes. I keep my paw on the outside of the crate bars. My Human continues to pet me until I fall asleep.

I wake up a couple of times and the room is dark again. I feel lonely, but I smell her. My Human is beside me, lying alongside my crate. It's not as good as sleeping next to her, curled up alongside her, but the big feeling of emptiness and sadness doesn't come back.

Soon, the morning light streams through the windows. I wake up and shake myself off. Cleo is staring at me from across the room. She smirks and struts to my Human. Cleo kneads her paws in my Human's hair for a long time. When my Human opens her eyes, Cleo dashes out of the room.

My Human sits up and groans. She rubs her back. My Human should get a soft cushion. I feel great!

I wiggle and wiggle. My stomach growls as I place my front paws on the ground and stick my rear end up in a nice stretch. The Human laughs and lifts the latch of the crate door.

I tumble out and dash around the room in a game of chase with Cleo. She never lets me capture her, but I come close a couple of times before she dashes onto the couch and sticks her paw into me. Cleo has sharp claws on the end of her paw. I yelp.

My Human rushes over and checks me. "Cleo!" she scolds.

Cleo smirks at me before she swishes out of the room.

"Stormy," my Human says in a very sweet voice. "Breakfast." She kneels by a food and water bowl not far from my crate. I waddle over to the bowls. I'm glad my Human has set my bowls near my bed! How nice of her!

My ears drop into the water bowl and she lifts them out for me. My face fits into the food bowl and I eat fast. I always ate fast with my littermates!

The food tastes different. It's not all liquid and soft food. It's crunchy and I chew hard. After I finish every bite, my stomach feels a little bit ouchy. I sniff for a good poop spot.

"No, Stormy." My Human carries me to the door where we came in last night. She places me in the grass.

I get a little distracted by the smells. I smell Cleo and birds and squirrels.

"Do your business, Stormy." My Human touches the grass.

I know what she means. My Breeder Human taught us to do our business.

After I poop, my Human claps her hands and in a high-pitched, excited voice tells me I am a good dog!

I strut toward her. Of course I am! I am going to be magnificent!

I want to explore the grass, but my Human scoops me up and places me back inside the house. There are lots of other rooms and stairs, but she takes me to the room with my pen and food bowls. The room is blocked off with chairs and Cleo jumps over all of them to get in and out of the room.

"I want to learn how to jump like you," I tell Cleo.

She leaps over a chair cushion. "I can't teach you," Cleo says. "Only cats jump."

I know that's not true. My family knew how to leap over poles in agility. Cleo doesn't know everything.

My Human sits on the floor and I sniff everything in the room. I try to sniff under the couch and chair, but I don't fit very well. Instead, I find a hiding place behind a chair. I lie on my belly and wait while my Human tries to find me.

After a while, my Human lets me explore other rooms. I try to go up the stairs because I can smell her up there. There are a lot of her smells up the stairs. But she blocks the stairs with those chairs. Cleo hops over the chairs and sticks her paw out through the banister.

"This is off-limits to you," Cleo purrs at me.

I don't think it's fair Cleo can go wherever she wants. I growl at her and she swipes her paw at me. I jump back. I don't want to get her claws caught in my head.

Cleo hops down the stairs. I follow her to a box with a lot of what looks like sand. She poops in the sandbox and everything smells so good. Cleo covers up her poop with the sand, but I can still smell it. As soon as she hops out, I stick my nose in the sandbox. I open my mouth to eat what Cleo has left, but my Human picks me up and shuts the door to the great treat sandbox.

"No, Stormy," she says. Her voice is firm and strong.

I obey her because I don't want to get in trouble on my first day.

But my Human can't keep the door closed forever. Cleo won't be able to get to her sandbox.

I will get some of Cleo's treats soon!

To read more of The World Is a Sniff.

Made in the USA
Columbia, SC
05 November 2024

45485554R00128